COMBUSTION

ISBN 978-1-7344402-0-1

Combustion

A reaction between a fuel, usually a hydrocarbon, and oxygen, which usually comes from the atmosphere. In the atmosphere the reaction takes the form:

$$C_xH_y + zO_2 + 3.77zN_2 \rightarrow xCO_2 + y/_2H_2O + 3.77zN_2$$

where $z = x + 1/4y$.

Most cases of combustion produce heat and light

After the Great Consolidation

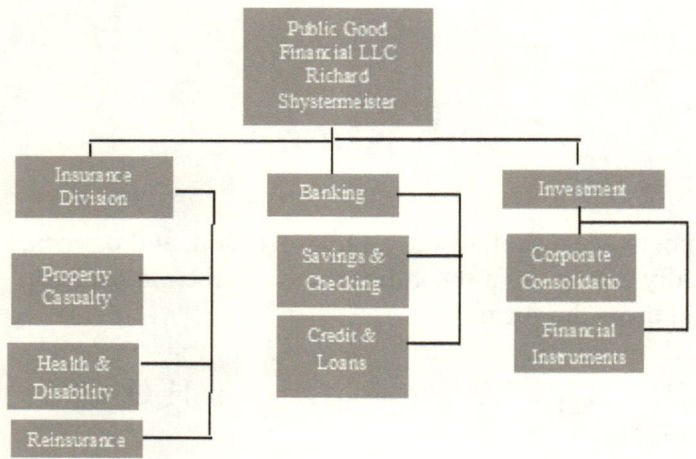

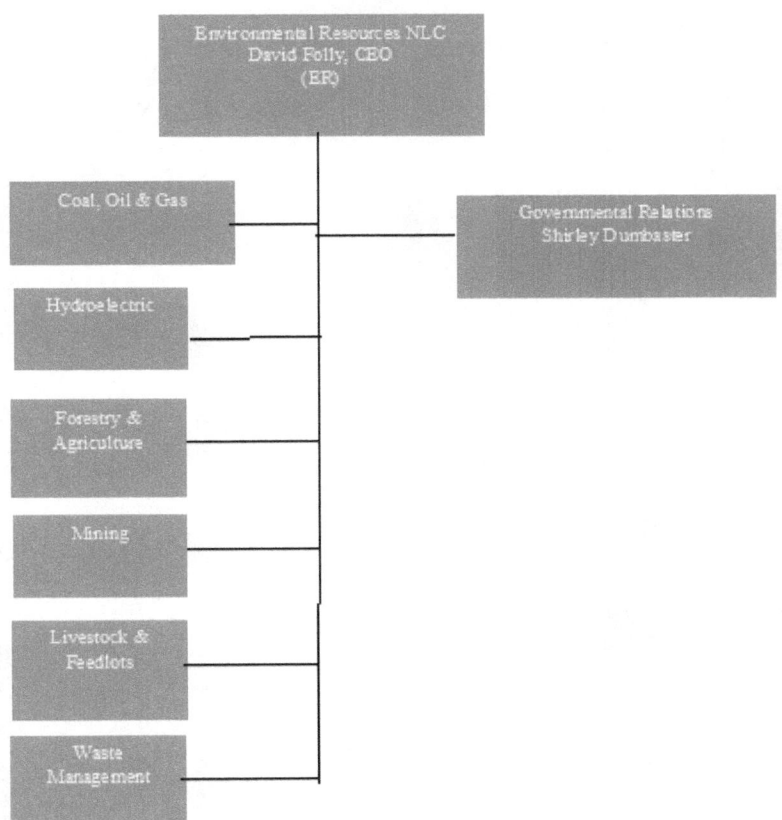

Environmental Resources NLC
David Folly, CEO
(ER)

Coal, Oil & Gas

Hydroelectric

Forestry &
Agriculture

Mining

Livestock &
Feedlots

Waste
Management

Governmental Relations
Shirley Dumbaster

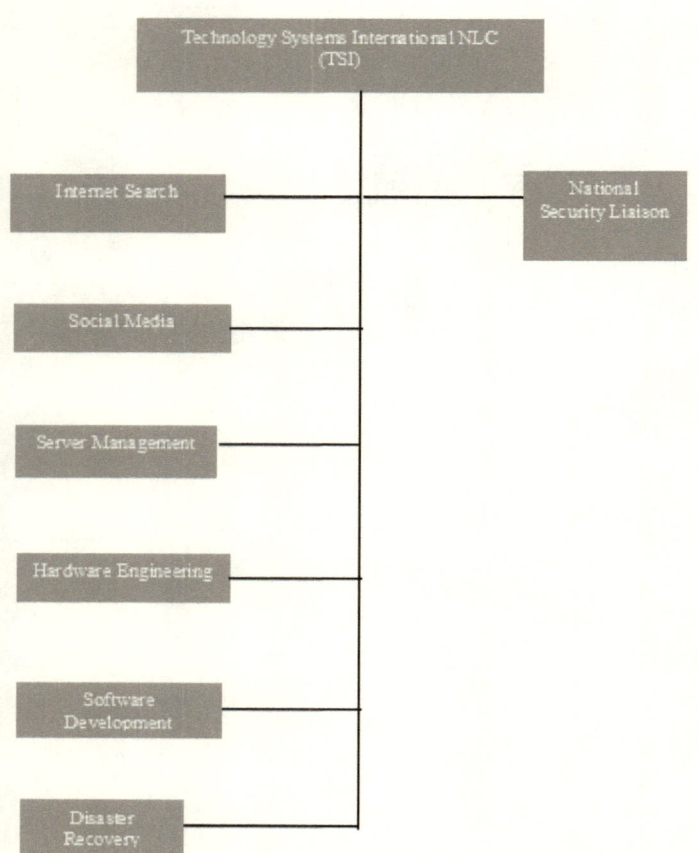

Technology Systems International NLC
(TSI)

Internet Search

National
Security Liaison

Social Media

Server Management

Hardware Engineering

Software
Development

Disaster
Recovery

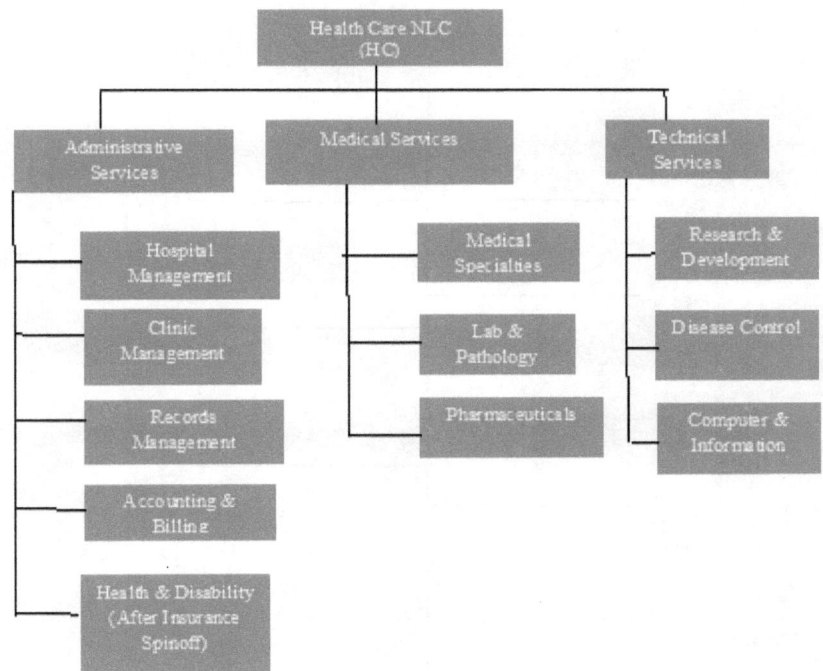

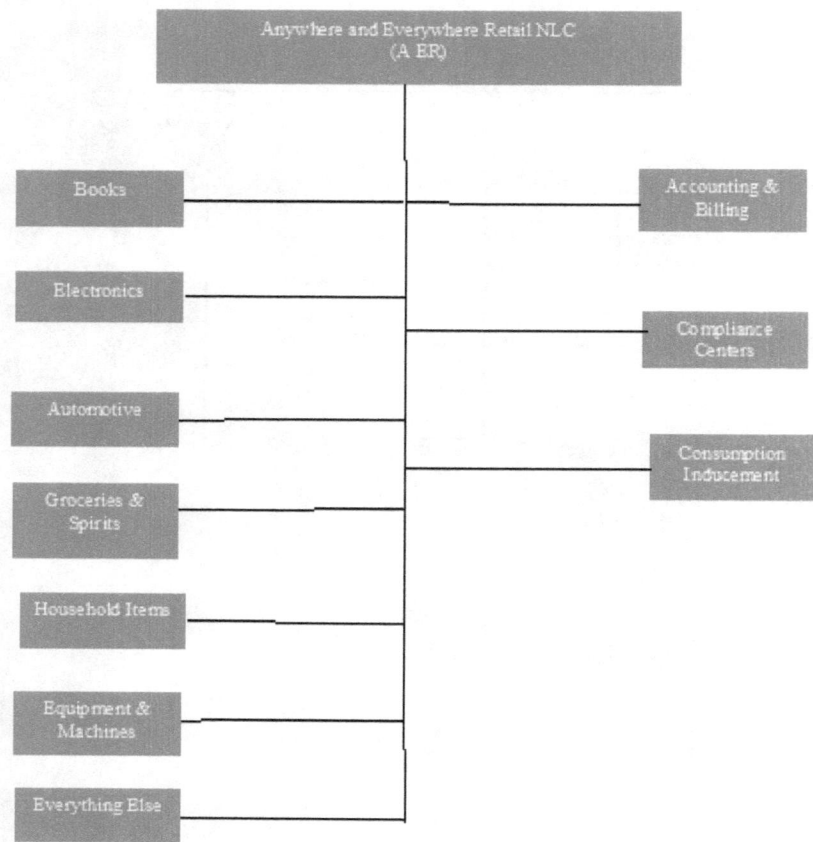

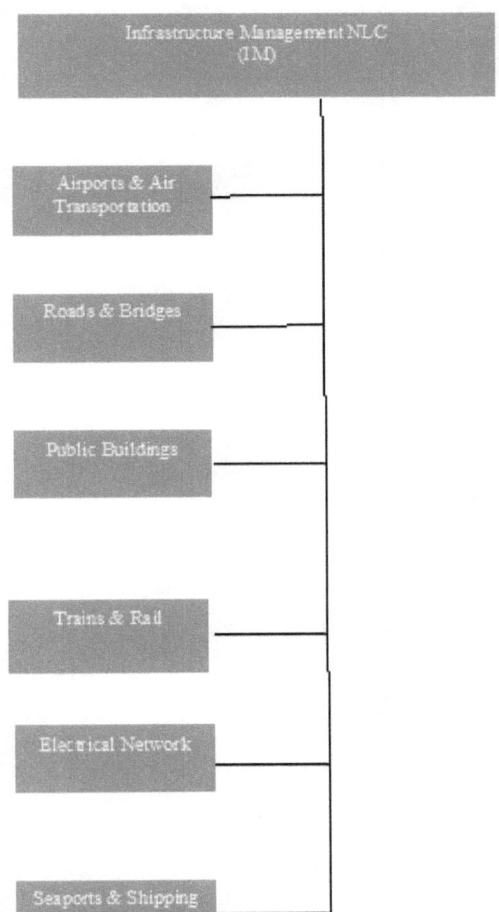

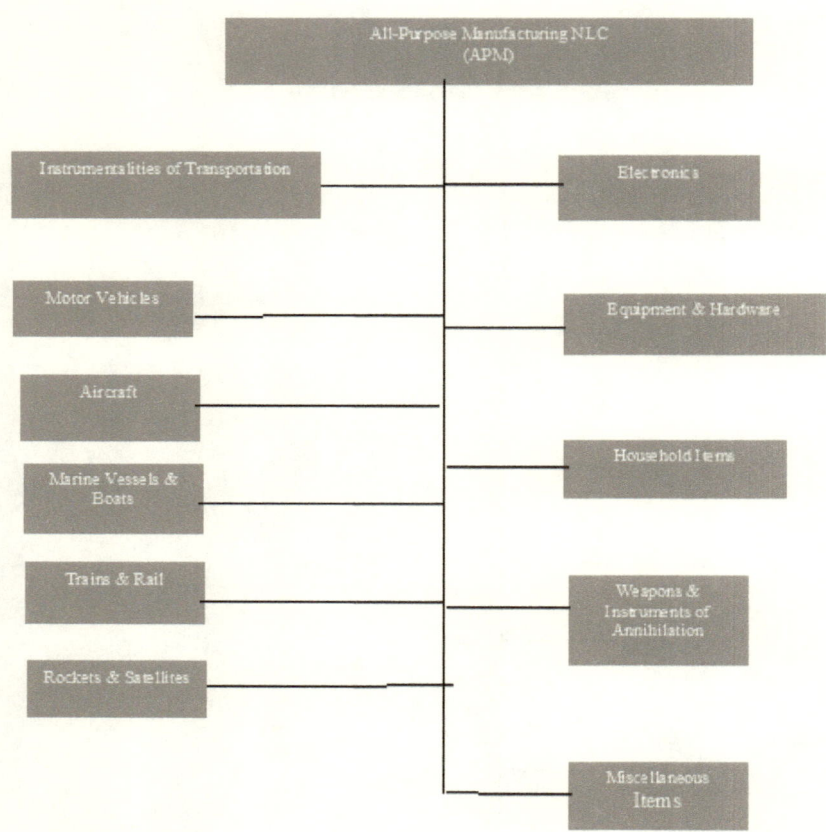

All-Purpose Manufacturing NLC
(APM)

Instrumentalities of Transportation

Electronics

Motor Vehicles

Equipment & Hardware

Aircraft

Marine Vessels & Boats

Household Items

Trains & Rail

Weapons & Instruments of Annihilation

Rockets & Satellites

Miscellaneous Items

10

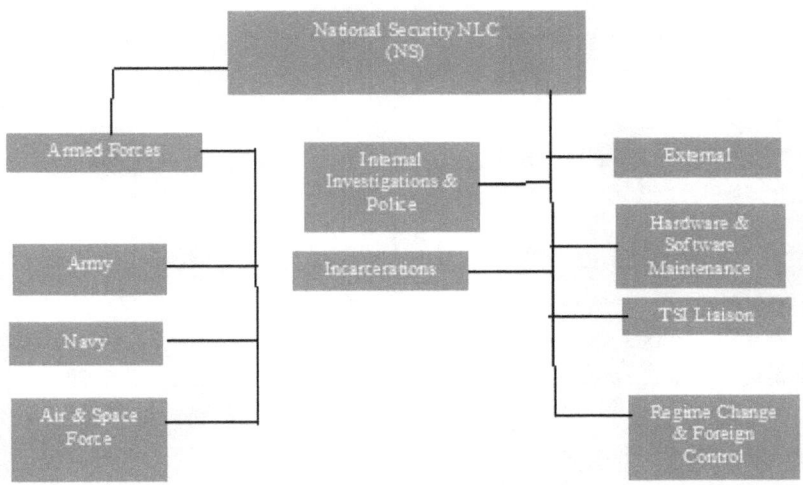

11

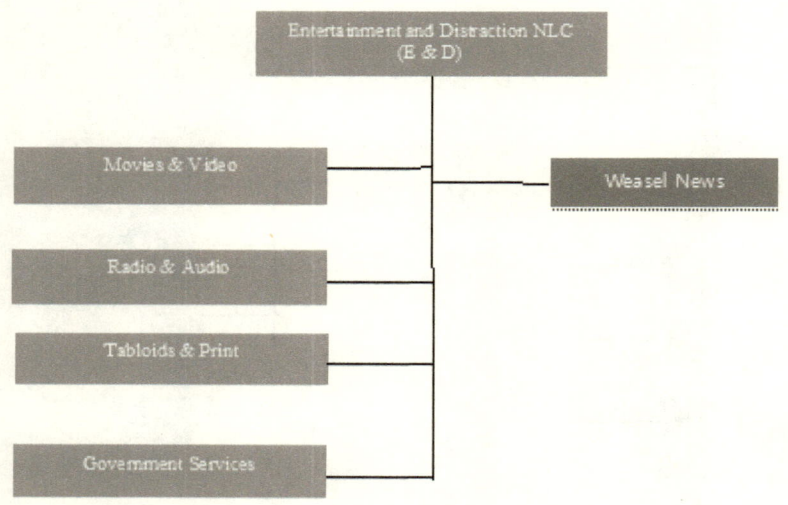

Prologue

Alex, in a state of semiconsciousness, was jolted into a more wakeful state by the dog whimpering. He suddenly remembered an obscure academic paper he read in the distant past, either in the Peace Corps or graduate school, he couldn't remember where. Elena seemed to be sound asleep next to him. His sudden remembrance of this paper angered him. It was largely ignored when it was published, but he now realized, although it was in the social sciences, and he was a natural scientist, it should have received serious consideration. It discussed various factors that had led to an increase in social entropy. Most of these were standard variables: political pressure, unintended consequences, racism, biomass reduction, inequality, etcetera. But his thought was focused on a new variable the paper had introduced. As he started to drift off into unconsciousness he became aware of Elena starting to feel cold. His last thought was *"Why didn't we pay attention to the rising tide of the asshole index?"*[1]

---

[1] This is a technical paper that Alex read about ten years after its publication during the Goldilocks administration. For the scientifically minded, this paper, and a portion of the discussion that followed its presentation, is provided in the Appendix.

First (Initial) Chapter

The sleek Space Odyssey Magnum Rocket sat on its launch pad at Cape Everlasting, glistening in the sunlight and waiting for the crew to board for the historic mission to Mars. The podium at the base of the mighty rocket was occupied by Jennifer Williamson, head of NASA, Eldon Ardhimer, CEO of Space Odyssey, and last, but by no means least, Donald McDonald, POTUS.[2] This mission was the culmination of years of effort to place the species *Homo sapiens* on the surface of Mars. Several robotic missions had been sent to Mars to provide a basic infrastructure for this crew to begin the process of claiming the planet for the United States which would require a permanent presence on the planet. The plan was to send rotating crews to the planet for a period of a couple of years until a permanent base could be established.

Ms. Williamson approached the microphone to begin the launch ceremony: "My fellow employees at NASA, Mr. Ardhimer and your employees at Space Odyssey, and above all, Mr. President: it is a great honor to be here to mark this momentous occasion. We are now about to embark upon our ultimate objective after years of intense preparation. We have learned a great deal from our moon missions and the preparatory missions to Mars. Now mankind is about to colonize another planet. Many individuals have been involved in this process. Unfortunately it is not possible to name them all, but I wish to express my deepest gratitude to my fellow employees at NASA who contributed so much to making this mission possible. I also want to thank Eldon and his employees for their contribution to this mission. It is my pleasure to

---

[2] Officially, President of the United States; beginning with the Goldilocks administration aka Posterior Orifice of the United States.

introduce Eldon Ardhimer, CEO of Space Odyssey whose momentous achievement stands before us here. Eldon."

"Thank you Jennifer. It was indeed an honor and pleasure to participate in this mission with you and your staff. Space Odyssey began as a humble support company that designed rockets and propellants for your missions to the moon. Over the years we've increased our engineering excellence, resulting in the Magnum Rocket that stands before us today. This technological marvel is about to take man to Mars and prove that we can not only survive, but also thrive in the harsh conditions that await us on the red planet. My company is deeply indebted to President McDonald for his vociferous support of private enterprise. I would like to ask Captain Wyzinsky to come to the podium for a few words and to introduce President McDonald. Captain Wyzinsky."

"On behalf of my fellow crew members, I wish to express how deeply honored we are to participate in this historic first manned mission to Mars. We are indebted to the employees at NASA and Space Odyssey[3] for making this mission possible. At this moment, I am also honored to introduce President Donald McDonald whose enthusiastic support for this project made the mission possible. Without his enduring support, despite sustained political opposition, we would not be here today. Please join me in welcoming our esteemed president, Donald McDonald."

"Captain Wyzinsky and your fellow astronauts, the staff at NASA and the employees of Space Odyssey and your families, and my fellow Americans: it is my greatest pleasure to address you on this momentous occasion. The mission you are about to undertake exemplifies the greatness of America and my leadership. Nothing comes close to the entrepreneurship of our magnificent corporations as exemplified by this great Magnum Rocket designed by Space

---

[3] Space Odyssey is a division of National Security NLC.

Odyssey and built by All Purpose Manufacturing. History will record that it was my persistence that made this mission possible, and future generations will forever recognize the sacrifice you are about to make in spreading the greatness of America to the alien world of Mars and throughout the solar system. By electing me as their president, the American people have finally unleashed their true entrepreneurial potential which this historic mission symbolizes. My greatness is their greatness. Onward and upward. Our thoughts and prayers are with you as you bring America to Mars."

The crew then boarded the elevator for the ride up to their module. The crew asked Captain Wyzinsky, "How could you stand kissing McDonald's ass like that?"

"I really had no choice. We all know that he will probably fuck up the entire planet and that he is using our mission to glorify his ego. Even though it is a propaganda exercise for him, at least we will no longer be affected by his absurd policies and corruption. Hopefully things will improve by the time we return."

At this point the astronauts strapped themselves in for the countdown and launch. Within minutes, the Magnum fired its engines and the rocket lifted off for the seven-month voyage to Mars.

Alexander Clearhead sat in the employee's lounge at the headquarters of NOAA watching the launch. *This is all bullshit,* he thought. *Why are we wasting resources to pollute another planet when we can't take care of what we have? Ever since the Goldilocks administration, we have been in decline. And now we have that asshole McDonald,*[4] *and these resources*

---

[4] Donald McDonald was a pampered brat born into wealth in Palm Beach. His grandfather achieved great wealth by exploiting the rain forest of Brazil. He would begin by logging off a certain area and then exploring for minerals. If none were found, he could convert the land to cattle ranching. If

should have been used to clean up all the damage we have done to our planet.

---

any minerals were present, he would set up a mining operation. These resources were fed into China's voracious appetite for economic growth. Even though all of this was illegal, timely payments to President Pompispaco kept his operation running smoothly. McDonald's father invested his inherited wealth in the creative financial instruments invented by Wall Street and real estate. Even though he was successful, the financial regulations at that time pissed him off and he decided to groom his son for politics.

Although his family did not value education, McDonald's father realized that in order for his son to succeed, he must have some academic credentials. An anonymous donation to Yale took care of this, and the aspiring Donald was accepted into the class of 2025 and he was promptly accepted into the Society of Skull and Bones. His academic performance was mediocre, but this didn't matter. His father wanted him to attend law school after graduation because this was the best ticket to politics, but the young Donald has no such interest, so his father persuaded him to go to Los Angeles and take up acting. This was the second best option.

The young Donald wasn't cut out for acting either, but he did discover that he had a talent for talk radio. He learned rather quickly that he could develop a lively interaction with his audience by expressing anti-government, free-market views. After several years on radio, he returned to Palm Beach and ran for mayor. Although unsuccessful, his father used this experience to teach his son the art of verbal obfuscation. He also used his influence to obtain name recognition for Donald by persuading the governor to appoint him to the vacant Senate seat that had resulted from the abrupt resignation of Senator McCoy.

Donald was verbally active in the Senate, ranting against government interference in business and raving about abortion. These views endeared him to Speaker O'Donnell. He produced no legislation, but name recognition was achieved, and he decided to run for president using the campaign theme "Make America Virile Again." This required the support of the Republican establishment, which he achieved by befriending Mickey Dense and persuading him to join the ticket. Without this asset, his run would not have been successful.

Next Chapter

Paul Burns arrived at his office in a state of apprehension. He was reviewing the division's loss ratios and was worried about reinsurance. After the consolidation of all major financial institutions into Public Good Financial, the insurance division had the combined function of primary insurance underwriting and reinsurance. The fact that the insurance division had to insure itself was the source of Paul's agitation. The loss ratios had been increasing at a steady rate over the past several years, and the damage from the rupture of the tailings dam and the explosion in the underground mine in northern Minnesota this past year had placed great financial stress on the reinsurance sector. Paul was also worried about the pressure he would receive from the independent agents in the field who would be demanding answers about reinsurance at the upcoming CPCU[5] convention in Honolulu. He buzzed his secretary and asked her to summon Andrew to his office.

"Andrew, please sit down and help yourself to some coffee. We have a big-time problem with these loss ratios. Your sector is being stressed beyond its limits, in large part because of the consolidation of all finance into one organization which requires us to reinsure ourselves, and the added stress from that mining disaster may bring us to the breaking point. Whoever thought you could insure a mining operation in the wet climate of northern Minnesota had to have his head up his ass. Because of the consolidation, we ended up with exposures that are essentially uninsurable. I have no idea how to handle this, and I am pissed off that Environmental

---

[5] Chartered Property Casualty Underwriter. The CPCU Society is an insurance industry trade group.

Resources continues to be profitable at our expense. Our immediate need is to develop a plan for the convention where you will be in the hot seat. I don't understand how we can afford Honolulu under these circumstances."

"We can't, but these conventions are planned years in advance, and a place like Honolulu is a motivator for the agents in the field to become CPCUs. We are expecting a large attendance this year. How has the investment division been doing? Perhaps they could help us."

"Now that most of the corporate consolidations[6] have been completed, that sector will be reduced considerably which will save some costs. Possibly we could get Financial Instruments to provide us with some backing. They are quite creative in designing obscure financial investment products, and they might be able to come up with an investment product and market it to the public. It would be a reinsurance bond type thing, but they would have to call it something else. I'll contact

---

[6] Economic activity had been becoming concentrated in fewer and fewer entities for a long time, but the process accelerated with the Goldilocks administration. A major achievement of that administration was the passage of the Corporate Entity Independence Act. This act essentially conferred a special form of citizenship on the nine major conglomerates that control 90 percent of the economy. The act freed these major entities from any future liability and governmental regulation. (Insurance is the assumption of liability by the insurer so the Insurance Division of Public Good Financial was the only entity that had liability exposure.)

These nine conglomerates controlled financial services, natural resources, technology, health care, retail, infrastructure, manufacturing, national security, and entertainment. For all practical purposes, these entities controlled the economy and most of government. The National Institutes of Health and the CDC were subsumed by Health Care NLC. Education was left to the states where it languished from the lack of proper funding and the term "free press" came to mean whatever Entertainment and Distractions NLC meant it to mean. At this point in history Environmental Resources NLC, through the efforts of Mickey Dense and the services of Shirley Dumbaster, had the most direct influence and control over President McDonald .

Dick this afternoon. If this works out it will give you some cover at the convention. But I have no idea what we will do in the long run. Our exposure is way too great. Let's meet again later this afternoon after I find out if Dick can help."

"Andrew, I talked to Dick. Come over to my office." Andrew entered the office after a few minutes.

"What did you find out?"

"I explained the situation to Dick and emphasized the fact that you needed a plausible cover for the convention. He is not sure that he can provide cover but suggested that you explain that we are working on it. You don't want the agents to panic. He is thinking that we will need to drastically increase the premiums because it is obvious that natural and manmade disasters are increasing. If push comes to shove, Dick doesn't know what will happen. Just explain to the agents that we understand their frustration and we may have to raise premiums. This will piss off their customers, but we are running out of options. Since the convention is in a few days, why don't you take the rest of the week off? You will need to be well rested to face the agents."

"Thanks Paul, I really appreciate that."

Andrew arrived at the convention well rested, but that did not last for long. The reinsurance section had overflowing crowds of very anxious agents. After Andrew's presentation and suggestion that the agents raise premiums, the questioning was relentless. Agent after agent explained that their customers were already at the breaking point with their premiums. This was true across all lines, from homeowners to businesses. Many felt that they might be forced to go out of business. Andrew was as sympathetic as possible and explained over and over that Public Good was working on the problem of reinsurance. His sympathy did little to mollify the agents. That afternoon he returned to his room too exhausted to enjoy the beach and needed to recuperate before the evening's festivities.

This is all bullshit, he thought before drifting off into a restless sleep.

Next Chapter

Two days after his return from Cape Everlasting, President McDonald held a rare news conference. But first he orchestrated an elaborate military parade to celebrate the successful launch to Mars. All nine of the major corporations had floats that illustrated their contributions to the effort. These were lined up in descending order. HealthCare and Public Good Financial were at the rear because they had no tangible items to put on display. All-Purpose Manufacturing and National Security were near the front because they could display their finest instruments of mass destruction and genocide. However, Environmental Resources was at the very front because this was McDonald's baby. The rationale was that the exploitation of environmental resources made all the other instruments of destruction possible. These floats circulated the Mall for hours to the tune of martial music, inflating the presidential ego.

When the parade finally ended, the president began his news conference. "Ladies and gentlemen of the press corps, we are on our way to Mars. This mission will extend American greatness throughout the solar system. It would not have been possible except for my economic leadership. No one can compete with our corporate giants, especially Environmental Resources and Technology Systems International. Thanks to me, we have the greatest economy ever created by man.

"You have just observed the finest military hardware on the planet. Let me assure you that our military strength will allow us to keep all these other little pipsqueak nations under full control. If we ever have to offer a deal to any one of these inferior states, let me assure you it will be a deal they cannot refuse. Because of my keen executive ability, we are in firm control, and with this mission to Mars we are masers of the universe. I will now take your questions so long as they show due respect."

"Mr. President, Paul Rudd from the *New York Truth and Fact*. Congratulations on the successful launch to Mars. You report that the economy is doing well, but there are rumors that people are having trouble finding affordable insurance. Can you comment?"

"I have not heard these reports myself, but I am sure that Public Good Financial has the situation under control. As I said, we have the greatest economy ever created."

"Mr. President, Amy Whitecoat from the *Wall Street Corporate Reporter*. I understand that you think the economy is doing great, but there are rumors that Infrastructure Management is having trouble obtaining loans. What can you say about this?"

"That has to be fake news. My economic policies, especially those getting rid of the corporate income tax, have propelled economic growth to new heights. I don't know why Infrastructure Management would even need loans. They have great financial strength from their user fees."

"But Mr. President, there are reports that users are having trouble paying the fees, and that their revenue is down at the same time that they need to repair damage from the recent storms."

"All I can say is that those reports are rumors, the source of all the fake news on the internet and in your papers. Our economy is great."

"Mr. President, Paul Rudd again. "Those recent storms and the increase in natural disasters in general, are the reasons behind the unaffordability of insurance. Agents in the field are saying that reinsurance is unavailable, and without reinsurance, the actuaries cannot come up with rates that are affordable. This is affecting homeowners and businesses alike."

"I know that there has been an increase in storm damage, but this really helps our economy. Having to repair all that damage increases GDP and keeps people employed. I don't know where all this negativity is coming from."

"Mr. President, Mark Wallace of the *Washington Policy Analyst*.[7] I understand that the breach of the tailings dam in northern Minnesota[8] is putting a strain on the insurance division of Public Good. This is a liability that they had to assume when Environmental Resources acquired the mines from Metals Forever. These are mines that never should have been approved in a wet climate, and now they have polluted the Boundary Waters Canoe Area which has destroyed the tourist economy in northern Minnesota. They have also polluted Lake Superior near Duluth. What is Environmental Resources doing to clean up this mess?"

"Environmental Resources is a great organization. It will do what is right, and again, fixing a situation like this contributes to GDP and economic growth. And the Boundary Waters Canoe Area was a waste of resources. Why should an area like that be set aside for a few stupid canoeists? Now that

---

[7] These three newspapers maintained their independence from Entertainment and Distractions on free speech grounds. The Supreme Court held that *Weasel News* could not be the sole source of news coverage. It would make news conferences too boring.

[8] After the great consolidation ER acquired two mines in northern Minnesota. One was an open-pit copper and heavy metal mine. The ore was extremely low grade, consisting of over 99 percent waste, containing sulfur and heavy metals, stored behind an upstream dam. The dam burst, spilling this shit into the Embarrass River (it lived up to its name) and ultimately the Duluth harbor, which was rendered useless. Then there was an explosion in the mine under Birch Lake which fractured the overlying rock and sent the same nasty pollutants into the BWCAW which poisoned the lakes of the BWCAW. This required the emergency evacuation of the canoeists using the area, and no one could enter thereafter. Forest Service personnel monitoring the situation reported that the odor of rotting fish and wildlife was unbearable.

it is polluted, we can use it for timber and additional mining. Wow, look at how GDP will jump when that happens."

At this point James McMaster, the presidential press secretary, saw that the press corps was becoming restless, which started to agitate the president, so he intervened.

"Members of the press, we have achieved our objective here today which is to celebrate the Mars mission. You have not asked a single question about this marvelous event. And you are certainly not showing respect to the president for this achievement. We are not here to discuss fake news. You know that our economy is doing great, so why are you raising these irrelevant questions? If you want to learn about the Mars mission so you can educate your readers about this event and how it makes America the greatest nation of all time, you can refer to the information we have posted on TheTruth.gov."

This action on the part of the press secretary really upset the members of the press, which resulted in shouts for attention and additional questions. Since this increased the president's agitation, James McMaster called in an aide to mollify the press while he expedited the president's exit.

When they returned to the Oval Office, James said to the president, "The first lady is busy in the East Wing. Why don't you go to your quarters and I'll summon Shirley? She will be here in a few minutes and I'll make sure the first lady remains occupied."

Shirley Dumbaster, who arrived in fifteen minutes, had been highly regarded in her profession before being hired by Environmental Resources. She was the sole occupant of the office of governmental relations at Environmental Resources. At the age of thirty-five, she was in her prime, and she maintained a discreet office a block from the White House. Governmental relations was an extremely important function at Environmental. She needed to be available whenever there was an eruption of presidential agitation.

Immediately upon her arrival, James escorted her to the presidential quarters and returned to his office. Shirley entered, and the president locked the door. Sensing his agitation,

Shirley knew exactly what to do. She removed his shoes and socks and then unbuckled his belt, removing his pants and underwear revealing the presidential cock, which she gingerly stroked until it stiffened. Then she gently sucked its head and skillfully twirled her tongue around it. Before it could come, she stopped and waited until it started to lose its stiffness. She repeated this procedure several times before sucking with vigor and taking his come in her mouth.[9] Once the president was de-agitated, she summoned James on the private phone and was

---

[9] Pussy licking is a major recreational activity for many men. Unfortunately, as people age, their necks become arthritic, which limits their ability to enjoy this activity. McDonald had a very active tongue which was well known from his speeches at rallies. However, he was severely limited in his ability to employ it for recreational use. The neck pain became severe as soon as he started to use it in this way. He was so frustrated by this that he had ordered Health Care NLC to do a research study on men's necks in search of a treatment.

The reciprocal function in women was not studied because women are not suitable research subjects. This research was unsuccessful as far as his case was concerned, but his personal physician finally determined what was the matter. McDonald, as was well known, spent a lot of time watching *Weasel News* which served two major functions. The first was to keep his conservative base entertained with complex conspiracy theories. The second was to massage the presidential ego with daily appraisals of his fine leadership skills. The fact that he didn't have any didn't matter. These daily appraisals captured his rapt attention and as he sat there watching, he extended his head forward toward the screen. This put severe pressure on the posterior portion of the spinal disk between C3 and C4. This induced a condition of cervical radiculopathy. His physician suggested the obvious which did nothing other than pissing McDonald off.

Shirley did not experience arousal when she performed her de-agitation services; rather she found the presidential cock to be rather grotesque. However, she was a professional and could skillfully go through the necessary motions. In addition she took comfort in the fact that she was performing a patriotic duty for which she happened to be highly compensated. She was relieved, therefore, that the president's neck condition kept his tongue off her pussy, but she did have to put up with penetration from time to time which was uncomfortable because of the size of the presidential member.

discreetly escorted back to her office, where she recorded the specifics of her services to the president. These reports were very important at Environmental Resources.

While the president was being de-agitated, McMaster's aide made a valiant attempt to mollify the press corps. They were not happy with this attempt.

Next Chapter

Various members of Congress were getting complaints from their constituents about declining gas mileage that their auto dealers and mechanics could not explain. They brought these complaints to Congress where they ended up in the hands of Mike O'Donnell.[10]

O'Donnell didn't know where to go within the bureaucracy to get a response that would appear to have some

---

[10]Mike O'Donnell was born into a solidly Republican middle class family in Louisville. He attended the John C. Calhoun High School where he excelled in debate. He didn't care what the topic was as long as he was victorious. This "win at all costs" trait intensified as he grew older. After high school he joined the U.S. Marines which turned out to be a mistake. He had hoped the culture of the marines would allow his masculinity to flourish, but his drill sergeant harassed him constantly and his masculinity felt like it was becoming feminine. This would not do, so he appealed to his father, a U.S. senator of little distinction, to get him an early discharge. However his experience in the marines instilled in him a deep appreciation for hierarchy. He vowed never to let himself be at the bottom of this structure again.

After his misadventure with the marines O'Donnell enrolled in Analorbits University where he majored in political science. He specialized in political rhetoric which served him well as he went on to get his degree in law. While studying law he met Clinton McClintock on a very casual basis. They would meet again in the Senate. After receiving his law degree, he obtained a coveted clerkship with the esteemed Rubin Macintyre on the Supreme Court. Macintyre taught the budding O'Donnell the art of political and legal obfuscation. After his clerkship O'Donnell ran for mayor of Louisville and lost. He was not cut out to be an executive. Immediately after this loss he ran for Congress and served a single term as a representative and then ran successfully for the Senate where he climbed the ranks and became majority leader. He attained the pinnacle of hierarchical success, and his control of the Senate was absolute.

truth, even if it didn't. Any report that had the potential to become controversial had to pass through his office. O'Donnell, being the majority leader in the Senate, had absolute control over that body and considerable control over the House as well.

He thought about this for some time and eventually came to the realization that since this issue involved cars, and cars are bought and sold on the market, it must involve commerce, and since it involved commerce, the Department of Commerce must have some answers. He sent his request over to that department.

When the request arrived at the Commerce Department, it filtered its way down through the bureaucracy. So far down that it ended up at NOAA, which wasn't an official government entity, even though it did receive government funding that the government knew nothing about. Once at NOAA, the request fell on the desk of Alexander Clearhead.

O'Donnell told Commerce to send him a copy of the report once they completed it and to keep a copy securely in their files hidden from view.

Next Chapter

Alexander Clearhead was the chief scientist at NOAA. At age forty he was in the prime of his career. He received his undergraduate degree in biology with an emphasis on ecology from Amherst College, and after he graduated he joined the Peace Corps in Indonesia where he helped develop sustainable fish farms. Upon his return, he received his PhD in climatology from MIT. An avid outdoorsman, he was lean and fit and was just beginning to show some baldness. His wife left him for another man after ten years of marriage which distressed him greatly. She had wanted children, but he was adamantly opposed to the idea because he believed that overpopulation was a serious problem that was leading toward environmental collapse.

He thoroughly enjoyed his work at NOAA because it gave him the opportunity to work on solving the problem of environmental degradation. Fortunately his agency had been left alone to work in obscurity. Since it was part of the Commerce Department, the administration didn't notice it at all during their restructuring of the government. Although it was unofficial and unrecognized, the administration also overlooked the fact that it still received funding. NOAA had been collecting data on the climate, the atmosphere, and the oceans for many decades. After the abolition of the Environmental Protection Agency, NOAA received the data that agency had collected, the receipt of which was unknown to the rest of the government. As chief scientist, Alexander had complete access to this data. He also had direct communication with the crew of the International Space Station which was kept running so the government could claim that it was still supporting science. Maintaining this facade for political purposes provided Alexander the opportunity to do his work without hindrance.

After watching the launch to Mars, Alexander had a meeting with Elena McPhee, the head of the Integrated Ocean

Observation System. Ever since his divorce, he had been attracted to Elena. He first met her when he was a senior at Amherst and she a freshman at Mount Holyoke, where she obtained an undergraduate degree in biochemistry and went on to get her PhD in oceanography at the Scripps Institute of Oceanography. She also joined the Peace Corps after obtaining her PhD and served in India where she assisted in the development of graduate programs in oceanography. The oceans around India were highly polluted, and flooding in coastal areas was common. She hoped these programs would help the Indians deal with these problems. She'd started her career at Woods Hole before Alexander persuaded the director to hire her five years ago. She was an athletic woman of thirty-five with a slim but firm physique, very attractive breasts, and shoulder length brunette hair. An important attribute in addition to her attractiveness was the fact that she was single. Elena had been analyzing data on ocean acidity which was the reason she'd requested this meeting with Alexander. They met in her office.

"Alex, I know that atmospheric CO_2 has remained steady for the last decade or so, and that the oceans have acted as a buffer. In addition to the general pollution from agricultural runoff and other polluted waters entering the ocean system and the buildup of plastics, fishing nets and gear and so forth, I am detecting an accelerating increase in ocean acidity. I am very concerned about the effect of this increase on the phytoplankton[11] at the bottom of the food chain. I would like to

---

[11] These microbes use photosynthesis to convert CO_2 to O_2. This important function is ignored by economists because it can't be priced. How do you put a price on a tiny little microbe? Without a price it, cannot be measured, and what is not measured cannot enter into the sophisticated macro-economic accounting models used in theoretical economics and in national income accounting. In fact most of the components of the biosphere are ignored for the same reason. It is theoretically possible to price cute mammals, but this does not make them economically relevant. The only

investigate further, but I don't have the resources. My staff has reported indications that the ecology of the phytoplankton may be changing. Do we have any allies in Congress that could obtain some funding?"

"Unfortunately, as you know, we are in a tight situation here. We get a minimum amount of funding which the administration seems to be unaware of. We don't want to call attention to this fact. The anti-science attitude in Congress is abysmal. NASA gets official recognition simply because space exploration is popular. The agenda of both the administration and the Congress is to maximize the misallocation of resources. We will pay a price for this. The only way I can think of to obtain funding is through one of the environmental foundations, but their resources are also stretched thin, and they are not allowed to contribute to the government, but there is one possible exception. The Mars Exploration Society is allowed to contribute to NASA. If we could persuade our allies in the nonprofit sector to channel money to NASA through MES, perhaps we could use some creative accounting to divert this to your department. NASA shares our concerns and will probably try to help if it can be done discreetly. I will bring your concerns to the director. In the meantime, if you can think of a way for your people to continue looking into this, by all means do so."

"Thanks Alex. I know we are in a difficult situation. If the ecology is changing, there may be organisms appearing that will need to be sequenced. That is the main reason I need additional funding. I'll also need some additional staff to do the sequencing."

---

parts of the biosphere where price is taken seriously are those parts that can be exploited for economic growth, such as agriculture, livestock, and lumbering.

Elena McPhee had a small staff, some of whom were located at strategic locations around the world. They were reporting some troubling trends that did not become apparent until their data was compared to the historical data from the now-defunct EPA. She had yet to receive any additional funding and brought her concerns to Alex before they went home for the night.

"Alex, have you heard anything at all about additional funding? The data I am receiving from my staff are pointing toward a serious trend. It appears that the pH of the oceans is increasing, as is the biochemical oxygen demand. I know we cannot discuss trends like this as caused by climate change, but I don't know what else it could be."

"Would you provide me with a summary of your data? Your data may help me with another issue that I have to look into. Have you noticed any decrease in your gas mileage? I haven't paid any attention to this, but Congress is hearing complaints about it, and somehow this request fell on my desk. The director thinks it came from the head of Commerce. I don't know what they want because they have no interest in anything scientific. I would like to say that it is caused by increased CO_2 in the atmosphere, but we don't have the data to back it up. CO_2 has leveled off. But this may be an opportunity to try to wake them up about global warming."

"I haven't paid any attention to it either, but now that you mention it, my mother has been complaining about her mileage. I thought it might be due to the fact that her vehicle is somewhat older than the average, but she has taken it to the dealer, asking about it. The dealer says that there is absolutely nothing wrong, but they have had similar complaints."

"That's interesting. I think your data might shed some light on this. I'm referring to what you said about biochemical oxygen demand. Your data might help me on this. I will take a look at it."

"Alex, I understand that you are a Unitarian. I haven't had any interest in religion, but your form of it appears interesting. However, I have trouble with your first principle: the inherent worth and dignity of each individual. Isn't that bullshit? How can you believe this? Isn't it evident that Socrates has greater moral worth than McDonald?"

"I know Socrates was a great philosopher, but he lived in ancient Greece which was a different era."

"I don't mean Socrates the philosopher—I mean, my dog, Socrates. McDonald is mean and snarly. As far as I can tell he has no moral principles whatsoever. The only thing he cares about is his ego. Socrates is friendly and joyful. He wouldn't hurt a flea. He doesn't have fleas, but he does get ticks when I let him run in the woods. They irritate him, but he tries to remove them gently. He is so successful at that that the ticks end up on me, and I have to dispatch them. And then there are so many other obvious examples. Hitler, Mao, etcetera, etcetera."

"I have to admit that I have trouble with that one also. We have an auction at our church, and one of the items is a sermon. By that I mean, if you have the winning bid for that item, you can commission a sermon on any topic. I have thought about trying to get that item at the auction to have our minister address that particular topic. I decided against it on the grounds that it would inflict cruel and unusual intellectual punishment on our minister. Do you really have a dog named Socrates?"

"Yes, I do. He is a spaniel poodle mix. He gives me the impression that he is thinking serious philosophical doggy thoughts. He flunked doggy school. At first I was disappointed, but I later came to recognize that was a sign of high doggy intelligence. He was rebelling against human authority. When you compare how we treat one another to the way dogs treat us, you will have to admit that, at least in some areas, if not all, they have a higher form of intelligence. At least a higher moral intelligence. Socrates, the Greek philosopher, was reputed to have a rather ugly face. Socrates the dog has a face that resembles that of the philosopher, but in his case, the face is actually cute, at least in my opinion."

"Sounds like quite the dog. I would like to meet him sometime."

"Sure. How would you like to come over for dinner this Saturday say around four?"

"I would love to. Thank you so much"

"I look forward to seeing you then."

This invitation induced great excitement within Alex's inner being. The fact that Elena named her dog Socrates only increased his admiration of her. He was hoping for an intimate connection. He also had a vague premonition, based on his work and hers, that there may not be a lot of time left to develop an intimate connection.

Elena McPhee lived in the Columbia Heights neighborhood of Washington in a townhouse on Harvard Street NW. This was a pleasant neighborhood with Asian restaurants and Meridian Park, where Elena walked Socrates. The park had an interesting fountain, historic statues, and an African style drum circle every Sunday afternoon. Columbia Heights was a short drive down Highway 29 from Alexander's house on Hemlock Street NW in Shepherd Park. Alexander was anticipatory as he made the drive. He arrived with a bottle of very fine wine and a trachea for Socrates. Before he could ring the bell, he heard Socrates barking up a storm. When the door opened, Socrates was jumping all over him.

"Alex, come in. Socrates, stop it. I apologize for his behavior. This is why he flunked doggy school." Alex didn't mind, and with Socrates on his hind legs, he gave his back a vigorous stroking.

Elena was wearing a sleeveless blouse with a matching short skort that emphasized her smooth white skin and shapely physique.

"I'm so glad to be here with you away from the office. I was in there earlier today, working on that report for Congress and looking at your data. It is very depressing, but I sent the report to the director."[12]

"I know it is. Let me show you around, and then let's take a walk. I think you will find Meridian Park interesting, and Socrates needs to get out and calm down. I think he likes you."

"I brought him a treat. I hope he likes it."

"Ick, what is that?"

"It is a beef trachea. I went to a pet store to get him a treat, and the salesperson said dogs really love them."

"Let's give it to him after the walk. I think he will need to eat it on the porch, however. It looks kinda greasy." Elena put Socrates's leash on, and they left for the park.

They wandered around Meridian Park at a slow pace so Socrates could sniff around and fertilize the various shrubs and trees that lined the walking paths.

"He sure likes to sniff a lot," Alex observed.

"Yes, he does. Did you realize that your olfactory organ has a surface area the size of a fingernail, but a dog's is the size of the surface area of his entire body? They have a very keen sense of smell."

"Wow, I didn't know that. They must have receptors for all kinds of molecules. What about their sense of sight and hearing?"

"Their hearing is much more acute than ours. I'm not sure about their sight. They are color blind, but if he sees a squirrel at a distance he tears after it if he's not leashed."

"How long have you had Socrates?"

"I got him when he was a puppy. At first I was worried about his intelligence. He managed to get his head stuck in a

---

[12] When O'Donnell received this report, he was pissed. This is not what he wanted. He said to himself, *This report will never see the light of day.* He decided to simply ignore this issue. His purpose was to represent corporations, not individual constituents.

yogurt container and couldn't get it out. Even after doggy school, I would call him, and he would just sit there staring at me. Eventually I realized this was a sign of intelligence. He wanted to prove to me that he has agency."

"Did you have trouble house-training him?"

"No. This may sound cruel, but I used a method called 'kennel training.' You leave him in his kennel all day long, but take him out about five times a day for a potty break. One of those times is also for a long walk. A dog won't foul his kennel which strengthens his bladder. I also used the classical music station on public radio to comfort him."

Socrates was turning out to be very useful for keeping their minds off their work. Their work was enjoyable and challenging, but what they were learning was scary and depressing. They slowly wandered back to Elena's place and sat out on her deck.

Alex opened the bottle of wine, poured two glasses, and gave Socrates his trachea. "I sure hope he likes it."

They both sat there in a semi-meditative state, watching Socrates devour the trachea. The wine was very smooth and soothing.

"How did you like India?" Alex eventually asked.

"I found it very depressing. I liked what I did at the university in setting up the oceanography program, but the country itself was divided between rich and poor. The rich were very rich and the poor very poor. It was also showing many signs of global warming. There were intense heat waves, then drought when there was supposed to be monsoons and, at other times, monsoons so strong that there was severe flooding. It is a very unpleasant place to live. I'm glad I had the experience because it opened my eyes to the environmental degradation we are inflicting on the planet. You were in the Peace Corps, too, weren't you?"

"Yes, I was in Indonesia. We were trying to set up environmentally friendly fish farming that would be sustainable. The idea was that we will need this if we are going to feed a growing population. However, the locals we worked with were looking for immediate results. We couldn't get the idea of sustainability off the ground. The government was very corrupt also. Like you, I was glad I went. The people were friendly and relatively easy to work with. But the entire country was converted to palm oil plantations. They had no idea how valuable their rain forests were. Now they are starting to suffer droughts with periodic heavy rains that just cause soil erosion. It's very sad. Jakarta is sinking, which will only get worse as sea levels rise."

Elena excused herself to prepare dinner, and Socrates jumped onto Alex's lap. "You are lucky to be a dog. You don't realize all the damage that we humans have done to the planet. Elena is right. You have more moral value than the assholes leading our governments and corporations."

Elena had prepared a simple but very delicious spaghetti dinner with a salad loaded with all types of different vegetables.

"You are one good cook. This is delicious."

"Thank you. I do like to cook. It helps me to focus on something creative. I don't regard our work as being creative anymore. All we seem to be doing is discovering more and more bad news."

"I feel exactly the same way. I thought that our findings would wake the government up, but they did the opposite. It didn't put them to sleep, but it made them openly hostile to what we were trying to tell them. Totally counterproductive."

"We just became another corrupt banana republic."

After dinner Elena served chocolate eclairs for dessert, and they both cleaned up the kitchen, went back to the deck, and imbibed a very smooth brandy with Socrates at their feet. Alex put his arm around Elena and drew her toward him, and after some deep kissing, began sucking on her earlobe. This got her aroused, and she led him to her bedroom where he removed her blouse, bra, and skort. He began sucking on her breasts, which were very fine specimens indeed, round, firm, and slightly smaller than medium size. He alternated between them, enjoying the firmness of the nipples. Then he began licking her stomach while working his way down to a lubricated vagina that had an enticing musky smell. He used his tongue to explore this area in detail, licking the clitoris, and then sticking his tongue in as far as it would go, and then licking the labia. Then he would suck on the clitoris and then lick the area around the vagina and lick and kiss her inner thighs. Then he went back to working on the vagina. He did this slowly for about thirty minutes, getting her aroused, then backing off, and then bringing her to a higher state of arousal until she experienced an orgasm that produced goose bumps all over her body.

All the while, Socrates remained still at the foot of the bed.

After Alex could sense that Elena was ready for more action, he undressed and inserted his erect member into her well-lubricated vagina and began a very slow in-and-out pumping action. Then he would stop. And then he would resume pumping. And then stop again. He did this for about another thirty minutes and then started pumping vigorously until they both experienced an explosive orgasm, which sent pulsations through her vagina that he could feel on his member as it delivered its cargo to its intended target. He pulled it out just in time to allow him to deposit the last few dribbles onto her nipples while he gently rubbed it in while licking her clitoris. This gave Elena a pleasant after orgasm.

At this point, Socrates got into the action by licking both of them.

Then they had another brandy before falling into a deep slumber.

In the morning, Elena made coffee which they drank in bed. Then she began sucking on Alex's nipples which immediately sent him into a state of arousal. Once aroused, she began slowly stroking his erect member, then sliding her tongue around its head, and then taking it deep into her mouth. And then stopping until his arousal calmed down a bit. Then she would repeat this process while gently messaging the area just behind his balls until he experienced an explosive orgasm and came inside her mouth. Elena enjoyed the taste of his semen. Socrates was nonchalant about all of this and remained half asleep on the bed.

They slowly got dressed, and Elena prepared breakfast.

After a breakfast of bacon and eggs they walked over to the Happy Souls Unitarian Universalist Church. After the service, and when most of the congregation had left, Alex introduced Elena to Elaine McDougal, the minister at HSUU.

"Elaine, this Elena McPhee my co-worker at NOAA."

"I'm pleased to meet you, Elena. I hope you enjoyed the service."

"I did. Alex has told me about his church, so I'm glad to finally visit it. It's right in my neighborhood, but I never had much of an interest in it. I like most of your principles, but the first one really bugs me. I explained to Alex that I think my dog Socrates has greater dignity and moral worth than McDonald. I just don't get that first principle."

"Let's grab a cup of coffee and go into my office."

After filling their caffeine receptacles, they went into Elaine's office.

"Elena, what is it about this principle that you find objectionable?"

"To be frank, I think it is total bullshit. McDonald has no dignity and moral worth whatsoever, along with the other obvious examples beginning with Hitler and running through Pol Pot. There is nothing inherent about dignity and moral worth; they have to be earned. People are not born with them. They have to learn them and practice them."

Alex interjected, "I have had doubts about this principle also. In fact, I was going to bid at the auction on the sermon of one's choice to address this issue, but I thought it would be too complex. Did you know that Dense[13] did his honor's thesis at Harvard on the sanctity of the unborn? His argument was that the unborn have equal moral worth and dignity, but once they are born, they are corrupted by social forces and their dignity and moral worth is compromised." [14]

"But that's bullshit too. Some people are just born evil, and social conditioning has no effect on them. Just look at how mean some little kids can be. And some of them never grow out of it. McDonald may have been taught his evil ways by his father and grandfather, but I'll bet his grandfather was born

---

[13] Dense was Harvard educated in political science as an undergraduate with an emphasis on conservative political philosophy under the tutelage of Harold Manchester, who reinforced his negative view of progressive government. As an undergraduate, his conservative views became increasingly reified, and he began to focus on abortion. His honors thesis was entitled "The Intersection of Fetal Viability and the Political Process." He then went on to get a degree in law and jurisprudence also at Harvard. His aspiration was the Supreme Court, where he hoped to end both abortion and government regulation, but at the time these views were too extreme for him to obtain the coveted clerkship at the court. He came from a lower-middle-class family that was constantly blaming the government for their lack of success, but he was a smooth talker, which impressed the admissions people at Harvard, and he was offered a full scholarship. Absent the clerkship, he obtained employment with the Republican Party and eventually rose to be its chairman. After several years in this position, he became a lobbyist for Environmental Resources.

[14] Abstract

Not only is fetal viability essential for social reproduction, but the fetus, since it is embedded in the womb, is uncorrupted by social forces. It represents the embodiment of God in human form. Once it exits the womb, however, it is immediately exposed to the corrosive social environment, and its God-given purity is immediately lost. This is known as the fall of man and has been substantiated by biblical authority. Here it is shown that any premature removal of the fetus from the womb, since it is pure form, is an offense against God and must be prevented at all costs, and the primary and most supreme objective of the political process is to protect the fetus.

evil. It's true that the unborn cannot do evil while in the womb, but the propensity to do evil is developing in the womb."

"Elena and Alex, this is, indeed, a complex issue, but the first principle is aspirational. It is not a statement of fact, but something to strive toward."

"But then why not say so, something like 'Human nature is ugly, undignified, and of questionable moral worth, but we aspire to eradicate these defects so that, in the long run, every human being will have equal dignity and moral worth.' But remember that John Maynard Keynes said, 'In the long run we are all dead.' If you look at what we are doing to each other and the planet, isn't it obvious that we have a very long way to go and we will all be dead before we get there?"

Alex was appreciating Elena more and more. Her sharp intellect impressed him. However, he also realized that Elaine's eighth amendment rights were being violated.

Elaine was in a difficult position. Unitarian Universalists are dedicated to rationality. And the very first principle of the faith was appearing to be very irrational indeed. How can you possibly rationalize the irrational? If you say that you have to take it on faith, you end up looking like an evangelical. And that doesn't look good. And it opens the door for all sorts of irrationality. Any crackpot can say, "I have direct access to God, and God tells me to keep all Muslims out of the country." Or anything else the crackpot wants done. Just take it on faith. And if you limit dignity and moral worth just to Unitarian Universalists, then you are engaging in discrimination, and that simply will not do. These things have to belong to everybody according to the first principle as written.

And it gets worse. Aren't "dignity" and "moral worth" culturally dependent? And worse yet, isn't their meaning dependent on their religious context? This is really, really messy.

Elena continued, "I am convinced that Socrates has greater moral worth and dignity than McDonald. Look at what McDonald has done. Where is there moral worth and dignity in casinos and golf courses? These things are trivial at best. On top of that there is anecdotal evidence that McDonald has raped quite a few women. And even though he is president and should be the one upholding the law, he won't release his tax returns, which probably means he is covering up criminal behavior. And on top of that, he is hell bent on destroying the environment. And he abuses our allies while he coddles up to dictators. How can anyone say he has dignity and moral worth? And look at what he has done to the migrants who are fleeing our war on drugs. Socrates, on the other hand, is friendly to everyone he meets. He greets them with enthusiasm and vigorous tail wagging. This makes people feel good. What I don't know is whether or not Socrates can distinguish between normal people and assholes. I have a feeling that he can. I can't imagine him wagging his tail in the presence of McDonald, but I don't know for sure. Maybe he would try to reform McDonald, but McDonald is beyond reform."

Elaine was in the uncomfortable position of not having a rational theological response. All she could do was to appeal to the power of love. But how can you possibly expect a rational person to love an asshole?

"I realize the first principle is very difficult to understand. It has a mysterious mystical quality about it, which is beyond the power of reason. Even Unitarian Universalists have to recognize the limits of reason and rationality. This is why it cannot be explained; it has to be felt. Humans are way more emotional than they are rational. So all I can do is appeal to your feelings. Your feelings of love."

This did not satisfy Elena. She had feelings of love toward Alex and Socrates, but she could not possibly imagine feelings of love toward McDonald. It is impossible to square a circle, geometrically impossible, against the laws of nature and mathematical rationality.

"I will have to think very, very hard about these mystical aspects of the first principle. I think I will come back. I really do admire your seventh principle." Elena let Elaine's love argument give her a graceful exit.

43

"You are a very bright woman. I do hope you will come back and join us. We are a very liberal, progressive congregation. You would be an asset to our spiritual quest."

"Thank you. I'll be back."

Alex and Elena left for the short walk back to her place. Socrates was very happy to see them.

Next Chapter

President McDonald was seriously considering nominating his vice president Mickey Dense to the Supreme Court. His vociferous opposition to abortion had Mike O'Donnell seriously worried, and he requested a secret meeting with McDonald which took place in the president's living quarters to insure secrecy.

"Mr. President, thank you for this meeting. I know that you are about to engage in your re-election campaign and that Mickey has been absolutely essential for your success. The power of his anti-abortion stance swept you over the top in the last election. However, I am extremely worried that if he is on the Supreme Court, he may actually outlaw all abortions under any circumstances whatsoever. I know that this is our party's position, but I need to emphasize the importance of not letting this happen. Dicky Dixon should have been impeached for establishing Earth Day and the EPA. All that did was encourage all those tree huggers to impose restrictive legislation on business. However he did two brilliant things when he was president before he was forced to resign which should have exonerated him. The first was his war on drugs. This destabilized most of Latin America and created many opportunities for military intervention and exploitation in that region. It also enhanced economic growth at home by increased enforcement and growth in the private prison industry. His other great achievement was his about-face on Title X, which provided federal funds for family planning, and he began campaigning on the sanctity of life. I must emphasize over and over that this was a master stroke of political genius. Without our stance on this issue, we never would have achieved the political success that we have enjoyed over many decades now.

"However, if Dense completely overturns abortion, our party is toast. This is the one issue that has held our base together, and once it is gone, we are done. I hope I have made

45

myself clear about this and that you understand how important this is for our political survival."

"Mike, I do understand your position, but I would not be here today except for the vociferous opposition to abortion that he brought to my campaign. I promised him the nomination to the court, and the party is expecting me to keep that commitment. You know how important this is to the rank and file and our base. If I go back on my word now, we could easily lose the next election."

"But if abortion becomes a non-issue, we will lose every election from now on. We must preserve some form of legality, or we have nothing to campaign on. You need to promise me that Dense will not allow any court ruling to go so far as to outlaw all abortions. We need to preserve its contestability where the states pass ever increasing laws restricting abortion, and the lower courts keep declaring those laws unconstitutional. No other issue unites our party like this one. People are beginning to turn against guns; they are losing favor with our overseas meddling and, absent this issue, they could start demanding that we bring back the welfare state. We cannot let this happen. Winning elections takes priority over everything."

"Mike, I cannot make that promise. Preventing abortion at any cost is Mickey's sole reason for being. I must go through with my commitment, and I cannot risk trying to influence how he will rule on any case. You know that that is still inappropriate. I do appreciate the logic of what you are telling me, but as they say, I am caught between a rock and a hard place. Mickey will be addressing the Ecumenical Right to Life Convention next week, and their support is necessary for our re-election, yours included. I do have a suggestion, however. You, or one of your people, could talk to Martha about this and try to impress upon her how important this is. She is the only one I can think of that will bring him around to your way of thinking. I cannot do this. Think how devastating it would be if my contacting her leaked out. You will have to be extremely discreet as to how you go about doing this, but it is much less risky for you to try than me."

"Don, that will be almost impossible. You know that I am on good terms with Mickey. What will happen if I get caught going behind his back? We need to find someone else who could do this. She would have to know that this is extremely important but not feel that the pressure is coming from us. And even so, we do not know that, even if persuaded, she will be able to influence Mickey."

"Well, give it some thought. Is she friendly with any members of your caucus? Any of your staff? I do hope you can indirectly bring Mickey around to your position. I know it is important."

"Thank you for hearing me out, Mr. President."

Mike O'Donnell left extremely dissatisfied with his conversation with the president. But as he was leaving the president mentioned something that O'Donnell knew was a major slip and he tucked this information deep into his medial temporal lobe. It explained why constituents were calling Congress about mileage. The president was highly agitated by the logic of O'Donnell's argument. So agitated, that he called for the services of Shirley Dumbaster.

Meanwhile in the far arctic there were several species of microorganisms that were doing this:

$$CO_2 + 4H_2 \rightarrow CH_4 + 2H_2O$$

These little buggers were keeping the atmospheric levels of carbon dioxide artificially low.

Next Chapter

Ever since NASA shifted its emphasis to the mission to Mars, its presence on the ISS was reduced to two astronauts. Polly Burman and Eugene Furman were stationed on the ISS for an extended stay.[15]

    "Gene, I just got an unusual request from Houston asking that we get in touch with an Elena McPhee at NOAA who wants any data we may have regarding the oceans. This sounds like something that is actually scientific, not the usual bullshit requested by the McDonald administration."

---

[15] Polly Burman and Eugene Furman were both educated at MIT where they met and then entered NASA's astronaut training program after graduation. Since they were both intelligent and relatively small, they were well adapted for living in the tight squishy quarters on the space station. Handling the scientific equipment in close quarters required a great deal of both intellectual and manual dexterity. Yoga and meditation training at MIT prepared them well for their future careers. In fact, they expected that viewing the earth from the space station would provide a highly satisfying meditative experience. Reality was a different matter.

    The Amazon basin and surrounding rain forest had been severely degraded by illegal mining, lumbering, and conversion of forest to grassland for ranching. Much of this was the result of McDonald's grandfather's voracious appetite for wealth, an enterprise that was the forerunner of ER. These environmental activities, supposedly illegal but officially sanctioned, had resulted in the gradual dehydration of the entire ecosystem. Fires throughout the region were common. This was all very obvious from the space station, but these observations got filtered out on the way down to earth by the political process, resulting in the perception of pristine environmental purity. Meditative tranquility was impossible when observing such destruction.

"That sounds great. Since you have been working with the Diatomeya[16] initiative, you should be able to provide her with interesting data. While you are at it, send her the images I have been collecting from the GEDI.[17] I have been extremely frustrated that there has been no official outlet for these images, which clearly document the destruction that has occurred in the tropical rain forests, particularly in Brazil and the Congo. Every time we pass over these areas, I get depressed. I hope NOAA can wake people up. I thought being up here observing the earth would be a pleasure, but it has turned out to be pure agony."

"I know how you feel. There is hardly any forest cover left in the Amazon. The clouds that used to provide rain have been replaced with smoke from fires, and the same thing is happening in the Congo. And all we can do is send the ISSAC[18] data from the Great Plains so McDonald can issue his bullshit reports."

When Elena received these communications from the ISS she, became depressed and cried. Her findings were confirmed.

----

[16] Stability of Geographical Position and Configuration of Borders of Bioproductive Water Zones of the world's Oceans Observed by Orbital Station Crews. This initiative involves the study of the biologically productive waters of the world's oceans.

[17] The Global Ecosystem Dynamics Investigation is mounted on the Japanese Experiment Module's Exposed Facility. This ingenious device provides laser imaging of high resolution observations of forest vertical structure on a global scale to quantify the aboveground carbon stored in vegetation and changes that result from vegetation disturbance and recovery, the potential for forests to sequester carbon in the future, and habitat structure and its influence on habitat quality and biodiversity.

[18] International Space Station Agricultural Camera.

Next Chapter

Richard Shystermeister sat in his office, mulling over the question of what to do about his insurance division. He had been forced to take over this function during the great consolidation, but he resented the fact that PGF was stuck with liability. It was because of this division that his company could not obtain NLC status and he was pissed. [19]

---

[19] Richard had been born into a family of bankers in New York City. Throughout his youth he kept thinking about money and how it could multiply. He literally saw visions of currency in his dreams, and these visions led him to study finance under the tutelage of the esteemed Ebenezer Moneyworth at the Wharton School where he focused on the economics of the multiplier effect. After graduation he traded financial instruments on Wall Street before joining the Bank of Wall Street. After the great consolidation he rose through the ranks of Public Good Financial and became CEO.

Ebenezer Moneyworth won the 2038 Nobel Prize in Economic Science for his work proving that vacuous money was essential for economic growth. To understand the importance of his work, you need to consider the history of money. Primitive money was denominated in trinkets and shells and could be called semi-vacuous. But when coins were introduced, it was possible to assign real value to money since the value of the coin was contained in the metal itself. When paper currency was invented, the valuation of money appeared to be problematic. However, if you examined any piece of paper currency, even though it was just a fancy piece of paper, there were symbols that provided a source of value. First of all, there were patriotic renderings in the portraits of the various presidents, kings, and dictators printed on the currency. These aroused intense feelings of nationalism, which provided a source of value. In addition, there were cryptic symbols and all sorts of numbers on the paper. Consider that pyramid with the mysterious eye. This obviously came from some secret cult. And the numbers, other than the number designating the denomination of the currency, were coded messages from other secret societies. Maybe they even contained national secrets in code. These symbols were an additional source of value. American currency had a very special attribute that provided even more value. It was sanctioned by God. It said so right on

Insurance was very distasteful to Richard. Although liability insurance was becoming increasingly obsolete, property losses were simply unsustainable. Insurance could not keep up with the increasing severity of storms and fires.[20] Although they were not part of his organization, he was worried that the insurance agents in the field could add a degree of misery to his otherwise comfortable life. But he did not want to prop up the insurance division with the profits from the other divisions of the company. There was only one

---

the currency. This was why the U.S. $ was used internationally as the official medium of exchange between banks. However this raised a serious economic issue. If the $ was sanctioned by God, it should never have lost its value. But the $ lost its value all the time as a result of inflation. This was one issue Professor Moneyworth had to deal with.

But now a much more serious issue had arisen. Tangible currency was becoming obsolete; replaced by electronic transactions and crypto currencies such as Bitcoin, which is computer code. Computer code is in the form of electrons. Now an electron is so small that it could be considered vacuous. How could you stamp the imprimatur of God on a thing as tiny as an electron? This was very important to distinguish an American financial electron from the inferior financial electrons of other nations. The technical issues involving electrons as money were the reason why so many physicists ended up in finance. Quantum mechanics deals with all sorts of quirky quarky subatomic particles. Some of these make up the electron. Physicists had found it extremely challenging to apply their knowledge of subatomic particles to the value of money. Ebenezer Moneyworth's work proved that even though money was vacuous, it was essential for economic growth. This work could not be explained in simple terms, and the technical details of the effect of the vacuity of money on the multiplier were beyond normal cognitive comprehension.

[20] There was a life insurance division in PGF, but life insurance had been declining for years. Life outside the womb no longer had much value. This was evident by the increase in suicide bombings, mass shootings and suicides, executions, mass incarceration, endless war, the war on drugs, environmental degradation, and antipathy toward the idea of social welfare, to say nothing of nuclear weapons. Life insurers tried to revive their business by offering fetal life insurance, but unfortunately this idea did not receive regulatory approval because of the obvious moral hazard.

solution to this problem. That was to spin off the insurance division. This was no easy matter.

Spinning off the insurance division was counter to the entire great consolidation movement, and it could upset an already increasingly fragile economy. Other than ER, TSI, and NS the other companies were losing business. People could not afford health care, manufacturing was sinking into the lower pits of hell, and retail was on the skids. This had an extremely adverse impact on the multiplier, and spinning of the insurance division would make it worse. It would also piss off Paul Burns.

Next Chapter

Environmental Resources was not only active in the Amazon; it was also in high gear in the Arctic. Its appetite for petroleum could not be satiated. It had petroleum extraction rigs throughout the Arctic Ocean and many more on public land and Indian land in Alaska. Bribes were necessary to gain access to the latter. All this drilling and processing created jobs so that McDonald could claim how effective he was in stimulating economic growth. It also produced a surplus, which did not help the price of oil. To control this problem, ER stored most of the oil in large-scale holding tanks. Since these were located in northern Alaska, they were more or less hidden from public view. This vast inventory was not reported in any official documents which allowed ER to maintain adequate pricing.

The extraction of oil also releases natural gas. In the past, this was simply wasted by flaring it off. Now, however, technology had been developed to pump it back into the ground for later use. However, the long-term stability of this process was unknown.

Since ER produced its own energy, it was efficient in all its other operations, and its CEO had amassed tremendous wealth, which provided him with several homes on each of the continents, jet planes, and yachts. He could have bought the presidency if he'd wanted it, but he preferred to enjoy his wealth in private. His control of McDonald was sufficient.

Before the great consolidation, David Folly and his brother Dennis Folly ran a petroleum company known as Folly Industries. In their early days, they lost a lawsuit brought by the government charging them with violations of environmental law. This loss pissed them off so much that they became active politically and vowed to get rid of the Environmental Protection Agency, which they did. After the great consolidation, Dennis retired to a life of ease. David however had been a major force behind the great consolidation, and he teamed up with Richard Shystermeister. They became masters of mergers, and they sat at the pinnacle of power.

Next Chapter

The former insurance division of PGF ended up in bankruptcy court before it could acquire a name for itself, so the court simply called it Irresponsible Insurance LLC. After the petition was filed, the effect of the bankruptcy had spread panic throughout the economy. This was a time of increased property damage due to the effects of the unrecognized global warming.[21] Now, homeowners and small businesses began to

---

[21] There was anecdotal evidence that increased heat was correlated with increased anger. Even though mention of "global warming" was proscribed by an edict of the federal government, creative social scientists decided to scientifically test this observation. What they came up with became known as "The Great Temper-Temperature Correlation" (G T-T C). Temperature was easy to measure. Temper was different. They devised a complex index that consisted of such things as road rage, school shootings, other random shootings, political animosity, family discord, number of demonstrations against this or that, and decreased church attendance. The correlation coefficient was .9876543210. You couldn't possibly get more perfect linearity than that.

Minnesota provided a clear case study of this phenomenon. In the past there was this thing known as "Minnesota nice". For example, Minnesotans were so nice that they welcomed foreign companies engaged in resource extraction with horrible environmental and human resource records to come into their state and destroy what little was left of the state's natural beauty. They offered them all sorts of breaks: no taxes, no royalties, and low insurance rates. This niceness was attributed to the state's natural beauty which was theorized to have a calming effect on the state's inhabitants. It was thought that the emergence of "Minnesota not so nice" was the exploitation of the state's natural resources for sale to China after the damage they inflicted led to numerous cases of severe nature deficit disorder. The original justification for all this exploitation was "national security." How allowing foreign companies to exploit resources for sale to China promotes national security was a closely guarded state secret. But now this hypothesis had been thoroughly demolished. The original niceness was the result of the state's cold climate, and the not so niceness was the

panic and withdraw their savings from the banking division of PGF. Panic can metastasize very quickly into a full-blown economic depression, which is exactly what started to happen. This crisis created fear in Canada.

The Canadians were very much aware of the paralyzing politics in the United States and they were afraid that there would be mass migration across their border. This fear mobilized them. A mammoth construction project was initiated on an emergency basis to construct a wall on their southern border with the Lower 48 and their northern border with Alaska. They made every effort to avoid the mistakes that the Americans had made with their wall.

The first task was to dig a fifty-foot-deep trench along both these borders. This trench was then to be filled in with concrete within which seismic sensors were embedded. The purpose of this design was to prevent tunneling under the wall; if such tunneling were to occur, it could be quickly detected. The wall itself would consist of an elaborate electrified wire mesh fifty feet tall. If anything or anyone came in contact with this mesh, a current would be generated which would immediately discourage any such contact. Thus, the Canadians had a one-hundred-foot wall. As an added security measure, a moat was dug behind the wall filled with razor wire. This effort provided an energetic stimulus to the Canadian economy, and immigrants, other than Americans, were welcome to work on the project.

However, Canada had problems. The first was the Great Lakes and the border lakes in Minnesota. The latter were so polluted from mining that no one in their right mind would try

---

result of increased heat from the unmentionable global warming, which not only caused the increase in temper, but also increased the destruction of other natural resources through such things as forest fires, fish mortality, and the extinction of the state's moose population.

to cross there. In the Great Lakes Canada sank a cable sensor that would detect any crossing. The only gap in these sensors was at Niagara Falls, which was a sufficient barrier in itself. When alerted by the sensor the Canadian navy had high-speed hydrofoils to intercept and destroy any immigrant invaders. This left thousands of miles of coastline. The Canadians requested the United Nations to provide an international marine border protection force, with Americans excluded, to protect its coastline. This request was hung up in the UN bureaucracy. A border wall in the Pacific with Hawaii was not feasible, and UN assistance here was included in the request.

The increasing market instability along with the unavailability of insurance was starting to induce a panic. It was clear to James McMaster that a presidential news conference was in order, but this would cause presidential stress.[22] He avoided this problem by arranging to have the

---

[22] Most males would find it virtually impossible to get an erection under conditions of stress. McDonald was different. He had a rare medical condition known as chronic stress-induced hyperactive erectile functionality. Under stress he would get an erection. In public this caused him concern because he worried that his erection might be visible which set up a positive feedback loop that increased his stress, which then enlarged his erection to the point where he thought it might rupture. Because of this condition, McDonald hated giving press conferences. At home, however, it proved useful in preserving domestic tranquility. If Mary started bitching at him for whatever reason, he would immediately get an erection, which led to a quick fuck with his wife, which, in turn relived the anxiety of both.

This condition also explained his well known tendency to welcome combat with his enemies, domestic and foreign. The press could not understand how he had the energy to engage in verbal martial arts on the internet late at night. They thought he must be on some sort of drug, but they didn't dare raise this issue in print, on the air, or on the internet. The real explanation, however, was that when McDonald was so engaged in creating self-induced stress, it produced a condition of erectile optimality: just the right amount of hydraulic pressure to produce just the right amount of turgor such that it was firm and stiff, but since he was in control, there was no danger of rupture. It just quivered with excitement in a state of

president appear on Weasel News where he reassured the public that there was no such thing as an economic crisis. Although the public believed McDonald's assertions of economic stability and growth, their behavior indicated otherwise. The press secretary was relieved, and the president remained calm. Although a visible erection in front of the press corps was avoided, the economy was by no means stable.

---

evanescent tumescence. This state of rapture would last hours, and if it got out of hand, he would have either take care of it himself or call in Shirley to take care of it for him. Because it was so rare, there was no medical or physiological research on this condition. It was assumed that it involved the dopamine receptors, but the cause remained unknown to science. McDonald may have been the only known case, but it was known only to his doctor who had to keep his condition completely confidential.

Before he became president, McDonald was engaged in all sorts of activities that wiggled across the border between legal and illegal corruption and criminality. This caused stress, and since this was before he had professional de-agitation services, he would relieve his stress by raping whatever woman happened to be handy and then pay her a generous sum to keep her mouth permanently shut. If it wasn't permanently shut, his behavior would become public knowledge, which would increase his stress even more and damage the progression of his career. McDonald always prided himself on the size of his penis, which he tried to make into a symbol of national pride during his campaign. In its flaccid form it, was the size of a large Polish sausage and his testicles were the size of the balls on his golf courses. Its size required special underwear to contain it, but if it started to enter the erectile state, it would become quite visible to others. However, its size was not a natural endowment. Shoving it into areas where it wasn't welcome set up an inflammatory condition that became chronic, and this inflammation increased its size dramatically. Remarkably, this inflammation did not interfere with its functionality.

Next Chapter

O'Donnell knew he had to devise an alternative plan. After he returned to his office, he placed a call to David Folly in Houston.

"Dave, Mike O'Donnell here. When are you going to be in Washington? I have an urgent matter that I need to discuss with you, but I don't want to do it over the phone."

"Actually I was planning on being there next week. I need to meet with the president, because he needs me to reassure him of our financial stability. He uses our results as a major indicator of the country's economic health. I also want to visit my daughter at AJBU."

"Great. Give me a call after you arrive and let me know when you have time to meet. This is an urgent matter and it will probably take some time to discuss."

After David's meeting with the president, he met with O'Donnell in his office.

"David, good to see you. How was your meeting with the president?"

"I assured him that we are in great financial shape. Natural resources are always in demand, particularly energy. What is it you want to discuss?"

"I don't want to discuss it here. Let's go to my house where we will be more comfortable."

O'Donnell told his secretary that he would be gone for the rest of the afternoon. They took the elevator down to the Senate garage and drove a few miles to O'Donnell's house.

"David, come in. Can I get you a bourbon?"

"Sure, thanks."

After O'Donnell brought the drinks, he asked, "David, have you seen your daughter yet?"

"No, but I will the day after tomorrow. She has a busy schedule until then, and I want to wander around the Mall tomorrow. I haven't had much time to do that."

"Great. Let me get down to business. What I am about to discuss with you involves your daughter. I know this is a major imposition upon you and her, but it is extremely important. I'll explain. McDonald is going to nominate the vice president to the Supreme Court, and when this happens, abortion will be outlawed. I know our party has been advocating this for decades. However, if this happens, we will lose the one issue that has held our base together which quite likely will make us a very minor party. I cannot let that happen. I tried to get this across to McDonald, but I don't think he is going to do anything. That is why I need your help.

"I believe your daughter is friends with Lindsey Dense at Andrew Jackson.[23] The only thing that might prevent Dense from outlawing all abortions is if his daughter became pregnant. I'm sure that with her background, she hasn't had sex.[24] If she were to suddenly become pregnant, Dense might

---

[23] Andrew Jackson Biblical University was established during the second term of the Goldilocks administration in honor of Jacksonian democracy which was the initial expression of the superiority of executive power. Executive power, according to biblical authority, was vested in the authority of Caucasian males. The university provided education to both males and females, but they were strictly segregated. Undergraduate men received executive power training. Undergraduate women were trained in the art of enhancing executive power by providing unlimited support to the male ego.

The university was renowned for its Department of Creation Science and its Institute of Enlightened Governance. The former was engaged in research to prove that the earth was created in six days with a day of rest on the seventh. This project required perpetual funding. Success would have been much greater in proving the opposite hypothesis, but in that case funding would have run out. The latter was established in honor of Jackson's conviction that Native Americans were utterly incapable of self-governance in any form. Its primary focus was on establishing the superiority of masculine Caucasian forms of governance. It also offered executive leadership programs for executive branch Caucasian males.

[24] Mickey Dense was very protective of his daughter's womb. So protective that he bought her a gun and had her take the NRA's highly selective

possibly reconsider an outright ban. I know this sounds crazy, but hear me out. If your daughter Nancy and Lindsey study together, Nancy could drug Lindsey and then manage to inject some sperm well into her vagina to get her pregnant. The sperm would come in a high-nutrient fluid to ensure their survival long enough until she ovulates. They would also be equipped with nanotechnology that will guarantee success at impregnation. The drug would be something she inhales from a piece of cotton that would induce temporary loss of consciousness and no memory of the event. These materials would be disguised to look like an insulin injection, and they could be disposed of in a bathroom that has a collection receptacle for material like this. I will explain to Nancy that this is a matter of national security, which it is. Let me get you another drink while you ponder this idea."

O'Donnell returned with two full glasses of Kentucky's finest bourbon, which had a very calming effect on both men.

David responded, "I think this is a very dangerous idea. Nancy is a very sensitive young lady who would have a difficult time doing that even if she was persuaded that national security is at stake. How are we going to persuade her that national security is at stake? Winning elections isn't exactly a matter of national security."

"By God, it is. If our party loses control of the government, the liberals will take over, and you know what that means. They will reestablish the Environmental Protection

---

training course on womb protection. His goal was to train her to be the first lady which meant that he not only had to guarantee her virginity, but also had to find a husband for her who was of presidential caliber. She was homeschooled in conservative Christian ethics and the etiquette of first ladyship. At Andrew Jackson, she majored in the Christian Duties of the Wife, with an emphasis on executive wifehood. Unfortunately this training taught her nothing about the sexual duties of executive wifehood, even though this was an important part of satisfying the executive male ego, but was also absolutely essential for the production of executive fetuses.

Agency, which will regulate your corporation. You will become liable again. They will sue the hell out of you. They will tax you. Do you want to pay a carbon tax? Do you want some dinky little asshole liberal telling you what to do? They might abolish your company all-together. Do you want that?"

David took a slow, very deliberate sip of his bourbon as he pondered this potential threat to his company.

He then replied, "Of course not. But Mickey Dense was our lobbyist. He has always supported us. Impregnating his daughter would be the highest act of betrayal. How can you think of such a thing? If he found out that we did this, he would wipe our corporation off the face of the earth. I don't care how much McDonald loves us. If we harm Dense, he will undo everything he has done for us."

"But if we lose the election, we won't be able to do anything for you. The flaming liberals will wipe your ass off the face of the earth. We won't have energy. Without energy, any shithole country could become a major threat. The liberals would take over all your resources. And what would they do with them? They would conserve them. By God, you can't conserve resources; you have to use them. God put them there to be used; used for economic greatness, used for military greatness, used for political greatness. We can't let this happen. This is an extreme national security issue. Patriotism demands that we do something about it."

"But harming Mickey Dense is unpatriotic. In fact, McDonald would consider it an act of treason. Can't you just persuade him not to nominate Dense?"

"I tried, but he didn't buy it."

"If he didn't buy it, why should I? And if I were to try to persuade him, I would lose his support. Right now, ER has control over McDonald, but getting into that issue is too touchy. Our control would evaporate. Shirley does a great job, but she can't cover every contingency. And our control is limited to our corporate interests, not everything."

"If the liberals take over, you won't have control of anything. We just have to make sure that the cause of the pregnancy is unknown. If we are careful, they won't know that we were behind it. If you think about it, you will realize that that is the lesser risk."

"Even so, I don't want to put Nancy in that situation. I don't think she is up to that sort of thing. She is in ladyship training, just like Lindsey Dense. And they are good friends. I cannot subject Nancy to that sort of trauma. Ladyship training doesn't prepare her for impregnation espionage. That involves technical skills, which are unladylike."

"I realize that, but we can train her once we persuade her that it is in the national interest. You have many technical employees who would be good teachers, even though this is a different technology than what they do."

"But if she does that, she will lose her lady attributes, and her education will be useless. She won't have a future."

"She won't have a future if the liberals take over. This shouldn't hurt her lady attributes; it will enhance them because she is serving the national interest. It will enhance her feminine mystique."

"But how are we going to persuade her that this is a national security issue?"

"I will work on that, and you can work on getting one of your employees to provide the technical training."

When it came to winning elections O'Donnell was very persuasive.

When it came to naiveté, Nancy Folly was very naive, a personality trait that made O'Donnell's task of persuasion relatively easy. He had to convince her way beyond any shadow of any reasonable doubt that what he was asking her to do was a patriotic act of the highest order. Nothing was more patriotic than preserving national security. He had to convince her that (1) abortion had to be kept legal in theory, but not in practice; (2) this was a classified state secret at the highest level of the classification scheme; (3) because it was classified, the Supreme Court could not be told about it even when they were considering outlawing all abortions; and (4) only the pregnancy of the chief justice's daughter would preserve national security. O'Donnell had to muster all the skills of his legislative persuasiveness.

Nancy Folly attended the Houston All-Girls Christian Academy from kindergarten through high school. Her education emphasized the biblical interpretation of nature, which was reinforced at home when her father impressed upon her the necessity of subduing the earth and extracting all its resources for the glory of God. He emphasized the fact that doing this made him very rich, which was direct evidence that God was very happy with his work. He needed this emphasis on God's happiness with him as a way to impress upon Nancy the necessity of aiding and abetting O'Donnell's national security agenda. He also had hopes that his daughter would become the first lady at Environmental Resources after his retirement.

After his meeting with O'Donnell, David Folly contacted his daughter at AJBU and made arrangements to go out for dinner at Flannigan's Steak House near the campus. After introducing her to some very fine wine, he began emphasizing the link between national security and divine providence.

"Nancy, as you know, God has been very happy with my work extracting natural resources for his glory. These resources are used for national security, and God wants us to have national security. And now you are going to have an opportunity to promote God's interest in national security. Tomorrow, you will be meeting with the highly esteemed Senate majority leader, Mike O'Donnell. He is going to give you an opportunity to save our national security. I cannot give you any details about this opportunity because it is classified. But tomorrow, Senator O'Donnell will explain it to you. But everything he tells you is classified, so you cannot discuss it with anyone, including me. I'll be making arrangements for your technical training which is on a need-to know-basis. Other than that, I know nothing except the fact that this is extremely important."

"Daddy, this sounds serious. Are you sure that I'll be capable of doing whatever this is? You mentioned technical training, but I don't know anything about technical stuff. Doesn't that have something to do with computers? I don't know anything about computers."

"It has nothing to do with computers. Your Christian education will give you the divine inspiration to pursue the technical training. You will do just fine as long as you remember that it is all for the glory of God and country."

The next morning David took his daughter for her meeting with Senator O'Donnell. He excused himself on the grounds that he was not privy to classified information, but he met with O'Donnell later that afternoon to discuss her technical training.

"Senator, how was your meeting with my daughter?"

"It went very well. I took her over to National Security, and they gave her a tour of the facilities, which really impressed her with the importance and complexity of national security. Then we went to a secure area where I was able to convince her that impregnating Lindsey Dense is a national security issue of the highest order. At first she resisted this idea as being un-Christian, but I was able to convince her that national security was necessary for the security of the kingdom of heaven and keeping abortion legal on paper was a national security issue. I was able to convince her that if all abortions were to be outlawed, there might be violence and attempts to leave the country, and because Canada has secured its borders, it would increase the violence even more, and that simply was not good for national security. It would be a sign of national weakness, and quelling internal dissent and violence would only encourage our external enemies, of which there are many. So now you need to make arrangements for her technical training."

"We have technicians who do a lot of engineering work on drilling and fracking, both of which are a form of penetration. I think I can put together a team that will be able to apply these skills to the art of penetration without visible evidence. Their skills in covering up the pollution they generate will come in handy, I'm sure. Spring break is coming up, and Nancy will be in Houston, so I'll have her complete the technical training then."

"Great. David, I really appreciate this. It's a shame that your allegiance to duty, honor, and country cannot be publicly recognized."

The technical training was thorough and very successful. It turned out that in addition to being naive, Nancy had delicate manual skills that came in very handy.

Next Chapter

Paul Burns was pissed. So pissed that he contacted the head of the United Insurance Agents of America and suggested that they organize a march on Washington. He suggested that all agents purchase matching black three-piece suits and women matching black jumpsuits. All agents should also carry matching briefcases. They should also construct four floats, the significance of which would become obvious.

The head of the UIA of A contacted the heads of the local chapters, and organizing began in earnest. The purchase of the attire for the occasion temporarily boosted the stock price of AER and APM. It took six weeks to plan the event. Although this appears to be a short amount of time to plan a demonstration of this magnitude, the fact was that the agents had nothing else to do, and they were angry as hell.

There were over two and a half million people employed in various aspects of the insurance industry. Most of these were employed by independent insurance agencies and brokerages. The rest had been employed by PGF until the spinoff. Organizing for the demonstration began before the insurance division could obtain a new name for itself, which was only important so that it could be a named party in bankruptcy court.

On the day of the demonstration most of these agents converged on the nation's capital city dressed in their matching attire. They came by bus, train, and plane. The floats had been assembled at a secret location and were ready one week before the demonstration. The National Park Service no longer estimated crowd sizes at Mall demonstrations, but independent estimates showed that it exceeded the record set by President Obama's inaugural crowd of 1.8 million. *The Guinness Book of World Records* had to add a new category for the most suits present at any one event. A new decibel record was also achieved. The previous record had been recently set at the

Ecumenical Pro Life Convention at the conclusion of Dense's rousing speech. These were very angry agents.

The demonstration began with speeches from the Capitol steps, the purpose of which was crowd arousal. Once aroused, the floats were lined up on Madison Drive NW for the procession down to the Washington Monument. The insurance agents had four mammoth floats. The first had a huge slot machine surrounded by scantily clad young women, the second a mock-up of the ninth hole of McDonald's Heavenly Hills Golf Course with balls everywhere, the third a rendition of his Wall Street Hotel with rats departing in all directions, and the fourth a model of the US Capitol with a screws being driven into its dome. The agents themselves were lined up in rows on the Mall. As they marched with their briefcases, they sang the following:

> *Old McDonald had a casino*
> *EIEIO*
> *And in this casino he lost many chips*
> *EIEIO*
> *With a chip chip here, and a chip chip there*
> *Here a chip, there a chip,*
> *Everywhere a chip chip*
> *Old McDonald had a casino*
> *EIEIO*
>
> *Old McDonald had a golf course*
> *EIEIO*
> *And on this golf course he lost his balls*
> *EIEIO*
> *With a ball ball here, and a ball ball there*
> *Here a ball, there a ball*
> *Everywhere a ball ball*
> *Old McDonald had a golf course*
> *EIEIO*
>
> *Old McDonald had a hotel*
> *EIEIO*

And in this hotel he had many rats
EIEIO
With a rat rat here, and a rat rat there
Here a rat, there a rat
Everywhere a rat rat
Old McDonald had a hotel
EIEIO

Old McDonald had an erection
EIEIO
And with this erection he screwed the nation
EIEIO
With a screw screw here, and a screw screw there
Here a screw, there a screw
Everywhere a screw screw
Old McDonald had an erection
EIEIO

Given that these agents had every right to be angry, this was a dignified demonstration. They had just lost the source of their livelihood without just compensation. In the not-too-distant past, there was this thing called a "social safety net" that provided minimal support in situations like this. Now such an idea was regarded as an evil anachronism.

Usually the police harassed demonstrators on the Mall. On this occasion they were restrained because of all the suits. It just wouldn't look right clubbing a suit. It was unknown whether or not McDonald, holed up in the Oval Office, heard any of this protest. He should have because of the decibel level, but the White House simply ignored the demonstration. After about six hours the agents dispersed; boarded buses, trains, and planes; and returned to their homes and offices. The hospitality sector of the DC economy enjoyed a two-day windfall as did the transportation sector now subsumed by IM.

Next Chapter

Since the financial crisis did not resolve itself with the president's reassurances, James McMaster confronted the president, telling him that he had to have a press conference to re-calm the public. McDonald hated doing press conferences for obvious reasons and decided instead to address the nation in a Rose Garden announcement nominating Mickey Dense to the SCOTUS. This announcement would deflect the public's attention from the financial crisis. He would use the financial performance of ER to assure the public that everything was just fine. It was McMaster's duty to assure that no questions would be raised. The president approached the lectern.

"Ladies and gentlemen, it is my great pleasure to nominate our esteemed vice president, Mickey Dense, to be the next chief justice of the Supreme Court. Mickey has served with distinction as vice president, and his constant concern for the sanctity of the unborn has earned him worldwide renown. He will make a fine chief justice. I urge the most rapid Senate confirmation.

"I know that some of you are concerned about the economy, but I am here to tell you that it is just fine. Environmental Resources has been having outstanding financial results. The resources it extracts from our productive earth form the basis of all economic activity, so the economy is in great shape. Have a nice day."

James McMaster quickly escorted the president from the podium, which prevented any possibility of presidential panic. The press corps, to say the least, were extremely pissed off. They wanted to know how the vice presidency would be filled. They wanted to know if the purpose of this nomination was to prohibit abortions under any and all circumstances, and they did not believe the economy was hunky dory.

Now the Canadians were not only worried about economic migration; they were worried about abortion migration. They rushed to complete their wall.

Next Chapter

Immediately after the nomination of Mickey Dense, O'Donnell called Clinton McClintock into his office. McClintock was the chairman of the Senate Judiciary Committee, and it was his job to shepherd the nomination through the confirmation process. McClintock shared O'Donnell's concern on the importance of keeping the abortion issue, if not well, at least alive. Electoral success depended on it. [25]

---

[25]McClintock was from Mississippi which was a very anti-abortion state. He needed to rail against abortion to win election, but he also realized that when he could no longer rail against it, his chances for electoral success fell off to near zero. He had no other competencies, and it was his constant support of O'Donnell that had put him where he was. He had a law degree from Analorbits University which was practically useless except for credentialing his chairmanship. It was at Analorbits where McClintock first met O'Donnell, but they didn't become close until they met again in the Senate.

Analorbits University was founded by Analus Orbitus in the tumultuous year of 1968 in Birmingham Alabama. It was founded on the principle that the Bible is the source of all knowledge. However there is a bit of a problem with this idea that the founder did not recognize. The Bible consists of two testaments: the old one and the new one. The old one is concerned with the Kingdom of the Jews. Its religion is Judaism. The new one is concerned with the Kingdom of Heaven. Its religion is Christianity. Since the new one came after the old one, this implies that Christianity evolved out of Judaism, but according to Christian evangelical authority, evolution is not allowed by God because God created everything including knowledge. How then do you reconcile these two different sources of knowledge?

The political science department at Analorbits had been involved in an extensive research effort trying to establish without a doubt that the US. Constitution was directly derived from biblical authority, and that therefore the United States was a Christian nation. This effort occupied the legal scholars at AU for a long time and it formed the basis of the political science syllabus. Both O'Donnell and McClintock were motivated to enter politics as a result of these teachings.

"Clinton, I am extremely worried about Dense. We have to support his nomination, but we must prevent him from prohibiting all abortions. I am now speaking to you in extreme confidence. Not a word of this is to leave this room. I contacted David Folly, who has a daughter at Andrew Jackson who is also a friend of Lindsey Dense. Without going into details, I was able to get Folly's daughter to impregnate Lindsey Dense, leaving no evidence of penetration whatsoever. I hope this pregnancy from an unknown source will force Dense to reconsider a total ban. I am sure that by now Lindsey must be showing some signs of pregnancy. During the confirmation hearings, you need to refer to this. He will wonder how you got this information. Before you hold the hearings, you will need to invite yourself to do a lecture on the role of the unborn in creation science[26] for her class. Then you can say that you noticed she might be pregnant."

"How am I to invite myself to give a lecture to her class?"

"Just call up the chancellor at Andrew Jackson and explain that you want to give a lecture on this subject because you need to get it out of your system before you hold the hearings, and it fits into Andrew Jackson's mission. Since you are a prominent senator, I am sure they will be happy to accommodate you."

"Are you sure that I will be able to see any signs that she is pregnant?"

"You will need to wait another month or so before you give the lecture. Schedule it now. By waiting, it will make it easier for them to fit you in to their schedule. I'll handle the delay in holding the hearings."

---

[26] All students at AJBU are required to take Creation Science 101.

Next Chapter

Six weeks later, Senator McClintock gave his lecture at Andrew Jackson. It was well received and he was awarded an honorary doctorate in creation science. He also noticed that Lindsey Dense showed the beginning signs of pregnancy. It was now time to hold the confirmation hearings. He knew that even though his party was in the majority, the minority Democrats would turn the hearings into a media spectacle. He would have to exert tight control over the process.

The hearings began the next day with the vice president's opening remarks:

"Senator McClintock and esteemed members of the judiciary committee: it is a great honor to be here before you today, and I wish to thank President McDonald for nominating me to be chief justice of the Supreme Court. It is the highest honor in jurisprudence. My views on the sanctity of the unborn are well known, and I am sure that you are eager to question me about them. Therefore, let me say at the outset that I cannot address any hypotheticals. As we sit here today, we do not know what issues will come before the court, and in the interest of judicial integrity, it is not permissible for me to speculate on how I might decide a case. Hopefully, your understanding of my position on this will keep these hearings to a reasonable length of time.

"The sanctity of the unborn is not the only issue likely to come before the court for resolution. As you know, the First Amendment has been under attack, particularly on our college campuses, where the failure to use proper pronouns and other forms of politically correct speech has resulted in expulsion from the campus. Again, even though the founding fathers would have been appalled by this, I cannot comment on hypotheticals likely or unlikely to come before the court.

"Since the abuses in environmental and business law have been corrected by your branch of government, the burden on the court has been lessened. That will leave more time for the court to consider other issues, and it will be my honor to apply my intellect in resolving them. I'll now take your questions."

"Thank you, Mr. Vice President. As chair of this committee I want to welcome you here. These hearings will be historic because you are the first vice president to be nominated to sit on the high court. In most other hearings, the nominee coming before this committee had an extensive decision record from their service on lower courts. You have no such record and the members of this committee will want to ascertain your judicial philosophy and this includes the issues you mentioned. I am somewhat at a loss as to how to proceed, given your reluctance to address hypotheticals. I do have questions about the sanctity of the unborn, but I'll reserve them for later. For now I'll turn it over to the minority chair, Senator Ornery."

"Mr. Vice President, welcome. I am interested in your remark about political correctness. What is taking place on our college campuses is downright ridiculous. But we must remember that this asininity would not have come about except for the fact that there is so much discrimination in our society. Rather than attack it on First Amendment grounds, it would be far better to attack the underlying discrimination. What are your thoughts on this?"

"To my knowledge, the word 'discrimination' is not mentioned in the Constitution, but free speech is. The job of the court is to interpret the Constitution. If "discrimination" is not mentioned in the Constitution, we have no way to ascertain the intent of the founders."

Senator Ornery continued, "Let's say an American Indian wanted to rent an apartment in New York City but was denied while a white person with exactly the same earning capacity and credit-worthiness was allowed to rent. Doesn't this violate the equal protection of the laws? And that is mentioned in the Constitution."

"You are raising a hypothetical, and I simply cannot comment on hypotheticals."

"I want to know your thoughts on equal protection. If we enforced the equal protection clause, these free speech issues on college campuses would not arise. We wouldn't be in the position of twisting the English language into absolute confusion with all these new identities for which there are no pronouns. And the people who can't stand it and speak out against it would no longer need to speak out against it and would not end up being expelled from campus."

"The Constitution does have an equal-protection clause, but it says nothing about discrimination. The purpose of the court is to give a strict interpretation of the Constitution. It says 'equal protection of the laws,' but we don't know the content of the laws, and since we don't know their content, I simply cannot comment, because laws with unknown content are all hypothetical."

"I am finding all this very frustrating. If we cannot determine your thoughts on constitutional jurisprudence, how can we possibly determine whether or not you can think at all? That makes these hearings superfluous and useless."

McClintock realized he was losing control of the hearing and interjected himself into the questioning.

"I think this line of questioning has gone on long enough. Let me turn it over to my colleague, Senator Able."

"Mr. Vice President, welcome. It is an honor to have you here today. Your efforts on behalf of the unborn are exemplary, so I will not question you about them. Instead, I want to get your thoughts on the Third Amendment dealing with the quartering of soldiers in houses. I find this amendment very confusing. It mentions that they cannot, without the owner's consent, be quartered in any house. But then it goes on to talk about times of war, and it implies that they cannot be so quartered in war time either. And then it says something about 'in a manner proscribed by law'. It also comes after the Second Amendment which is about the right to bear arms. The court has ruled that this right is inalienable. Now soldiers, by definition, bear arms. By allowing homeowners to exclude soldiers from their homes, doesn't the Third Amendment violate the Second? Without going into hypotheticals, what do you think all this means?"

"That is a very interesting question. The court has extensive rulings on the Second Amendment, but very few, if any, on the Third. In fact this question is so complex that I sincerely hope any cases raising this question remain purely hypothetical. You simply cannot have one amendment or article or section or clause of the Constitution contradicting another. The founders would not have allowed it. It cannot happen, and since it cannot happen, I can't comment any further."

"But the Third Amendment allows homeowners to exclude soldiers from their premises in wartime also. Doesn't this contradict the 'provide for the common defense' clause in the Preamble? Doesn't national security take precedence over everything else?"

"All I can say is that it is impossible for the Constitution to contain any contradiction. If any were there, the founders would have eliminated them before publication. The Constitution says what it says without contradiction."

"But if that is the case, why do we need a supreme court to interpret it?"

"The purpose of the Supreme Court is to protect the executive power from the legislative power. The founders knew that the executive power was supreme. The newly formed United States, prior to its independence, had been ruled by a monarchy, which is supreme executive power. That tradition had to be carried forward into the newly formed nation, or it would not have survived. You cannot provide for the common defense without supreme executive power. On that point, the founders were clear."

"Thank you, Mr. Vice President. I realize I subjected you to a harsh line of questioning, but I want to be sure that you will protect the Constitution. Your answers are most reassuring. You will have my support."

"Thank you, Senator Able."

"The chair will now recognize a minority member, Senator Feeble."

"Thank you, Mr. Chairman, and welcome Mr. Vice President. I have just one question dealing with the executive power. Article Two Section One says 'No Person except a natural born Citizen, or a Citizen of the United States, at the time of the Adoption of this Constitution, shall be eligible to the Office of President'. There is an ambiguity here. What is the difference between 'a natural born citizen' and 'a citizen of the United States'? As we know, citizenship is a very complicated issue. Migrants are crossing our borders hoping to become citizens of our great country, and some of them succeed in this endeavor. Some of them have children who are born here. I assume that those who are born here would be classified as 'a natural born citizen.' Does this confer eligibility to be president upon them? And if it does, doesn't this weaken the executive power? And if it weakens the executive power, doesn't this interfere with providing for the common defense? You just said that the Constitution says what it says without contradiction. If this is the case, how does it resolve this thorny definitional issue of citizenship? I think this needs to be clarified so that the executive power is not polluted with foreign influence, particularly foreign influence that was the result of illegal migration across our borders. It's bad enough that we have foreign influence in our electoral system. What does the Constitution say about this?"

Senator Sassy interjected, "Mr. Chairman, I think these issues were clarified by the Fourteenth Amendment."

Senator Feeble responded: "But if that is the case, then the Constitution cannot say what it says without contradiction. The mere fact that it has been amended means that it had to be corrected, and if it had to be corrected, it cannot say what it says without contradiction. Mr. Vice President, please enlighten us on this issue."

"The Fourteenth amendment has nothing to do with Article Two. Article Two deals with the executive power, and eligibility to be president is limited to citizens of the United

States who happen to be natural persons. Having an unnatural person occupy that office would enfeeble the executive power to such an extent that the whole constitutional edifice would collapse."

"Thank you, Mr. Vice President. I yield the balance of my time to Senator Sassy."

"Welcome, Mr. Vice President. We are indeed honored to have you here. As part of this honor, I must ask you a difficult question about contradictions in the Constitution. The question has been raised about amendments correcting the Constitution, which contradict the assertion that the Constitution is without contradiction. There is a very unusual situation within the amendments themselves. The Twenty-first amendment nullifies the Eighteenth amendment. How do you explain this if the Constitution is non-contradictory and not in need of correction?"

McClintock did not expect members of his party to be asking difficult questions, and he knew he had to regain control of the hearing.

"Senator Sassy, before we delve into that difficult issue, which may exhaust the vice president, I want to return to the issue of the sanctity of the unborn. He needs to address this issue while his mind is still fresh. I must apologize for bringing this issue up given the vice-president's well-known views on the subject, but as you said, the honor of these proceedings requires it.

"Mr. Vice President, how would the pregnancy of your daughter, a pregnancy of unknown origin, affect your views on abortion?"

"That is entirely hypothetical, and as I said, I will not deal in hypotheticals."

"But Mr. Vice President, I gave a lecture at Andrew Jackson to your daughter's class, and it appeared to me that she was pregnant. I did not have the opportunity to ask her about this, but if this is true, then my question is not a hypothetical."

This assertion gave rise to pandemonium in the room, which McClintock could not contain. After it died down he allowed the vice president to respond.

"All I can say is that that is impossible. My daughter has the highest moral standards, and she is in first ladyship training at Andrew Jackson. She could not possibly be pregnant."

Since it was near noon, McClintock called for a recess. In private, he suggested that Dense might want to consult with his wife to see if she was aware of any changes with their daughter.

The vice president returned to his office and immediately called his wife.

"Martha, have you been watching the hearings?"

"Yes, I have. I didn't want to bring this to your attention because it would distract you during the hearings. About a month, ago Lindsey came home because she was not feeling well, vomiting and that sort of thing. We went to the doctors at Health Care to see what was causing this. They were baffled at first, but soon discovered that she was pregnant. Lindsey claimed that this was impossible, that she never had sex with anyone. The doctors examined her carefully and determined that she could not possibly have been penetrated. They said her vagina has high-quality virginity. They simply cannot explain it."

"Good God, how am I to explain this in the hearings? It's unbelievable. I know Lindsey would not do something so stupid and immoral as to get pregnant. And you say the doctors confirm that she could not have been penetrated? I need to think about this for a while. I'll see you when I get home."

President McDonald also heard this news, and called his vice president.

"Mickey, I was as shocked as you were hearing what McClintock claimed. Is there anything to it?"

"Yes, Mr. President, there is. I just called Martha and she confirmed it, but the strange thing is that Lindsey didn't have sex with anyone. The doctors at Health Care said that her virginity was intact. They had no doubt about it."

"Try not to worry about it during the hearings. You have my full support, and if you need me to back you up, I'll do it. I suggest that you ask for a recess until tomorrow to give yourself some time to think about how to respond."

"That is a good idea Mr. President. Thank you."

Mickey Dense returned to the hearing room where the senators had already reconvened. His ashen face revealed that what they had heard was no rumor. He immediately requested a recess to the next morning which was granted.

When Mickey got home he immediately called his daughter who reassured him that she indeed did not have sex with anyone. He also called the doctors at Health Care who backed up his daughter's reassurance. He explained to Martha that he needed to be left alone to think about how he was to respond to this shocking news. He went into his study and entered a state of deep meditation. Then he retired for the night.

He woke refreshed the next morning, ate his usual breakfast, kissed his wife, and left for the resumption of the hearing. He appeared bright eyed and bushy tailed.

McClintock called the hearing to order.

"Welcome back, Mr. Vice President. Do you have anything you wish to say?"

"Yes, I do. Since I am under oath for the highest office on the highest court in the land, I cannot engage in obfuscation here. I will not get into the verbal trickery of saying I can neither confirm nor deny the assertion you made yesterday. I will speak the truth, the whole truth, and nothing but the truth. There will be no room for doubt, no room for ambiguity, and no room for qualification. I will be making a statement of fact—not opinion, just pure unadulterated fact."

With this assertion, extreme silence fell upon the room, and the senators sat motionless with bated breath. The vice president continued:

"Mr. Chairman, I was shocked to hear what you asserted yesterday. That shock intensified when my wife confirmed what you said. As you can imagine, such shock will disable clear thought, so I requested a recess. Now that my thought has clarified, I'll explain what happened. About a month ago, my daughter was feeling sick and she went home to consult her mother. The both of them went to the doctors at Health Care, the finest doctors in the land. They confirmed that she was pregnant and they also confirmed that she absolutely could not have been penetrated. They are totally mystified by this. So mystified that they have no explanation. Martha didn't tell me about this because she knew it would destabilize my thought process during these hearings. I dwelled on this last night in a deep state of meditation. There has to be an explanation for this. One of the things my daughter is studying at Andrew Jackson is creation science. They are engaged in deep scientific study of this subject. My daughter consulted her professors there about her mysterious pregnancy. They said there is only one possible explanation, and that is it must be a virgin birth."

With this assertion, a voluminous gasp erupted in the room. Since these hearings were televised live, this news spread through the internet and around the world within minutes. People went berserk. Within hours a wave of euphoria spread across the land, and up and down the Bible Belt various second coming and apocalyptic cults came oozing out of the woodwork, so much so that the woodwork collapsed. Since the property damage that resulted had no insurance coverage, the financial crisis intensified.

President McDonald was *really* impressed with his vice president's performance. It was simply brilliant.

O'Donnell, however, was sent into a state of shock. His strategy had failed, and he entered a state of depression that would later erupt in anger.

When Mickey arrived at home and after Martha congratulated him on his successful confirmation, she asked, "Do you really think Lindsey is having a virgin birth? I thought

Jesus's birth was the only virgin birth possible. Doesn't another virgin birth run counter to biblical authority?"

"No, not at all. The Bible was very clear that on Judgment Day, there would be a second coming where the righteous would sit at the right hand of the father and everyone else, sinners all, would be condemned to the lowest pits of hell."

"But Mickey, do you really take everything in the Bible to be literally true?"

"Of course. It is just like the Constitution. It is without contradiction. Its logic is infallible."

"But if that is true, why doesn't the Bible say anything about abortion?"

"It didn't need to. Abortions didn't exist. They were introduced by the devil after the Bible was written."

"How can the Bible account for something that didn't exist when the Bible was written?"

"Because the Bible made it very clear that anything the devil did was anti-biblical."

Martha was initially attracted to Mickey because his intense religiosity seemed so sincere. It was comforting to her. But as time went on, she had become increasingly uncomfortable with his absolute certainty about the literal truth of things that, to her, appeared more nuanced. Her daughter's pregnancy heightened this concern.

The next day her husband took his oath swearing to uphold the Constitution of the United States and was now chief justice. His long-sought opportunity had arrived. The office of vice president was officially vacant.[27]

---

[27] McDonald wanted the office to stay vacant out of fear that an occupant would prove to be more popular than him.

Next Chapter

Senator Mike O'Donnell was presiding over the Senate in the absence of the vice president. The Senate was having a heated debate on the Health Care Patient Privacy Protection Act.[28]

---

[28] This act was an extensive document of several thousand pages which covered patient privacy protection in health care. Most of it covered the history of health care. It was so thorough it went back to the time of Christ and his raising Lazarus from the dead. The first issue was whether being dead was a medical condition requiring treatment. If it was a medical condition requiring treatment, was Jesus a doctor? Many senators, since they were lawyers, argued that Jesus had to be some sort of legal professional. After all, he went around talking in parables. Wasn't this some form of legal interpretation?

This debate became quite intense, but in the end, since the equivalent of "Doctor," "Your Honor," or "Esquire" never appear in the New Testament, it was agreed that he was a divine version of both. Then, if he was a doctor, did he have a license to practice medicine? Even though he wanted to practice his profession, how did he know that Lazarus wanted treatment? He was dead, after all. Did Lazarus leave a health care directive? Raising someone from the dead was obviously a complex medical procedure. How could Jesus do this by himself? Didn't he need a health care team with modern equipment? If so, this made him a health care provider. Health care providers require compensation. Was Lazarus insured? And did Jesus have medical liability insurance? If he was insured, who provided the insurance?

Since Jesus was the Son of God, we can assume that God didn't want his son's business to fail, and therefore it was he who provided the insurance. It was unknown if and how Lazarus obtained health insurance. But the question here is whether or not Jesus, as a health care provider, was required to protect Lazarus's privacy. The purpose of insurance is to make the policyholder whole. Jesus could do this by returning Lazarus to the state he was in before medical treatment was applied. However, if Jesus did this, he would be charged with a highly felonious homicide. And what about God? Since God was the underwriter of Jesus's medical liability insurance, could God be sued? Obviously being raised from the dead is going to draw a lot of attention. Did Lazarus want this? If he was going to sue over this

Suddenly the sergeant-at-arms called a halt to the proceedings with the announcement that the Supreme Court had just outlawed all abortions. O'Donnell went into an immediate state of shock and had great difficulty maintaining his composure. Since there was loud shouting in the chamber, his state was not noticed. Once things had calmed down, which took quite some time, he adjourned the proceedings so that the members could return to their offices and study the decision.

---

issue, what tribunal would hear the suit? There was no division of powers like we have. Obviously, God was a legislator. This was clearly established in the Old Testament, where he issued the Ten Commandments and many edicts of prohibition and proscription. He was also an extremely strict enforcer, so he had executive powers, and he did pass judgments which meant that he had judicial powers. But his role as a monarch was never established until the New Testament, which introduced the idea of the Kingdom of Heaven.

Lazarus was in a real pickle. All he wanted was some damages and his privacy restored. But his lawsuit was before God who was author of the laws, enforcer of the laws, and interpreter of the laws. On top of this, he also had a vested interest in the case. The Senate staff did a diligent search of the legal literature, both scriptural and secular, to resolve these complex questions and came up empty handed. This was very frustrating for our poor senators.

In the end, the Patient Privacy Protection Act resolved this issue deep within the act itself.

§1B§a§2C§3b§4c§3A§6a§7cc§2bbb§1bbbbb§3B§5c§6aa§7b§15c: For the purposes of this Act, Patient Privacy is a commodity and Privacy Protection is a service for which any health care provider may charge an appropriate discretionary fee.

What was extremely unfortunate about this legislation was that it was a total waste of senatorial energy and hard earned tax payer dollars. The senators lost sight of the fact that there was only one health-care provider, Health Care NLC, and this provider could do whatever it damned well pleased. The question of whether or not God could be sued was unresolved, but it was clear that a corporation could not. In an era of fake news, it was understandable that our poor senators could lose track of basic facts.

And he did the same in a state of extreme anger. He told his secretary to take the rest of the day off so that he could be left alone undisturbed. He was livid. His office had a view of the Mall and his desk faced the window with that view. Behind his desk was a painting of General Robert E. Lee.[29] For a long time he just stared out the window at the nation's phallic symbol at the end of the Mall. Then he began pacing back and forth, back and forth. Eventually, he began pacing around his desk, clockwise for several minutes, and then counterclockwise for several more. This went on for quite some time.

Eventually, he sat at his desk and opened his computer to read the decision. Most Supreme Court decisions are laborious documents extending over many pages in extremely boring legalese. He expected the same, and was surprised how short this decision was.

Abrams v Miller et al. **663 U.S. 1028 (2058)**

The case before us involves one Shelly Miller and her doctor Dr. Alan Smith who have been sentenced to death by the State of Alabama for the abortion of her six-day-old fetus. Surgical Hardware, Inc. was also implicated because it provided the tools for the fetal extraction and was fined $1 billion. Under Alabama law, any abortion is punishable by death. The state court determination was appealed to the Eleventh Circuit (33 F.3d 1052 Judge Maxwell Evenhanded presiding) on the grounds of cruel and

---

[29] During the Goldilocks administration progressive liberals were furious about the display of confederate flags, statues of confederate political and military leaders, and other miscellaneous symbols of the confederacy. Their attempts to remove these items from public view resulted in an ultra-rightwing reactionary movement that resulted in the death of a progressive and injury to many more, acts of violence that led to very little incarceration. Although O'Donnell's painting was anathema to progressives, they could not be offended by its presence in his office because they were not allowed to come close to his inner sanctum and were ignorant of its presence there.

unusual punishment in violation of the Eighth Amendment cruel and unusual punishments clause. That circuit court vacated the decision of the state court. We heard the case under a writ of *certiorari*.

The facts of this case are not in dispute. The defendant was impregnated by her alcoholic father and sought an abortion from her co-defendant Dr. Smith, a neighbor and friend, who had to perform the abortion in his home since any abortion is illegal under Alabama law. Another neighbor witnessed the abortion and reported it to the local police, who raided Dr. Smith's home under a quickly obtained search warrant and arrested both defendants before the fetal remains could be disposed. The question before the court is whether their sentence violates the Eighth Amendment.

We take judicial notice of the following facts: under Pakistani law an individual may be executed for blasphemy, which involves mere words that offend the long-since-deceased Prophet Mohammad; in Afghanistan and India, honor killings are common because they preserve family values; our loyal ally Saudi Arabia uses hand choppings and beheadings to preserve executive monarchial authority; and prior to the formation of our great nation, the community of Salem was preserved from the horrors of witchcraft by hanging the witches. None of these acts are intended to inflict cruel and unusual punishments. Instead, they not only preserved family and community stability, they also purify the souls of the guilty parties so that they may eventually be able to enter into the Kingdom of Heaven.

We also recognize that abortion is a relatively modern phenomenon since the knowledge and tools necessary to carry out the act are of recent invention. Abortion is not mentioned in any of our founding documents. It is not mentioned in the Declaration of Independence, it is not mentioned in the Federalist Papers, and it is not mentioned in the Constitution. Therefore it is left up to our discretion to adjudicate this issue. We recognize that there is a rational state interest in preventing abortions, because abortion reduces population growth, and we need population growth to provide for the national defense. Applying the death penalty to abortion does not violate the Eighth Amendment because executing these poor souls will absolve them of their sin so that they may enter the kingdom of heaven.

Since the death penalty applied to abortion does not violate the Eighth Amendment and since capital punishment is applied to homicides, it follows that abortion is a type of homicide. Therefore the appellate court ruling is overturned and Alabama may proceed with the enforcement of its sacred law. It is left to Congress to apply this reasoning to the rest of the nation.

Our ruling is unanimous.
Mickey Dense
Chief Justice

After he read the decision, his anger reached the boiling point. There was no wiggle room here. Abortion was outlawed, period. The success of his party and his success personally in winning elections was about to be lost. Winning elections was O'Donnell's only objective. He didn't care how this objective was achieved.

Goddamn that fucking bastard! I told McDonald how important it was not to let this happen, and he went ahead anyway and appointed that goddamned Dense to the court. He repeated these thoughts over and over. Finally, he got up again and began more pacing around his desk eventually stopping to stare at the painting of Robert E. Lee. *What would he do in my situation? If he were betrayed by Jefferson Davis, what would he have done? Goddamn it.*

Receiving no satisfactory answer, he went to the cabinet in the corner of his office, retrieved Kentucky's world-famous product,[30] and poured himself a glass, and then another,

---

[30] O'Donnell's home state of Kentucky was famous for three things: world class bourbon, coal, and the Kentucky Derby. The latter recently became more of a detractor from the state's reputation after Marvelous Wonder, while crossing the finish line to victory by half a length, broke his leg and had to be put down. This raised a very contentious issue: The **Kentucky Derby Trophy** came with $2 million in prize money. Could this prize be awarded to a horse that was deceased? This issue was working its way through the courts.

Kentucky was a coal state, but there was no way it could outdo West Virginia in mountain top removal. So the "King Coal" title went to

and then another. Eventually this all kicked in and started to relieve his anger and he fell into a semi-conscious slumber which lasted quite some time. And then, deep within his cerebral cortex, some synapses fired and immediately he knew what he would do. His anger was resolved and he fell into a deep sleep facing the Mall with an SEG[31] on his face.

---

that state. But when it came to bourbon there was no question that the Kentucky variety was world class. Tennessee couldn't even come close.

[31] Vernacular: shit eating grin.

Next Chapter

There were only three people on the face of the entire earth who knew the truth, the whole truth, and nothing but the truth, and there was one who knew the truth, the partial truth, and nothing but the partial truth. The former were O'Donnell and David and Nancy Folly. The latter was Clinton McClintock. Nancy Folly became increasingly upset about her participation in causing all the ecstasy arising out of a virgin birth that she knew was not a virgin birth. Guilt weighed heavily upon her, so heavily that it put intense strain on her tender heart. Walking to class one day she collapsed with cardiac arrest. The best care that Health Care could provide did not save her. She was laid to rest in a private ceremony that received no press coverage. This left two people who knew the whole truth and one who knew the partial truth.

The death of Nancy Folly threw Lindsey Dense into an extreme emotional tizzy. This in addition to all the intense pressure from all the attention about her virgin birth. She paid a visit to her mother to try to seek an understanding as to what was happening. She was bothered by the fact that she didn't know how she became pregnant.

"Mom, I can't function. I am so upset about Nancy's death at the same time that I found out I am pregnant. I don't understand how I could be pregnant. I don't believe that I am capable of a virgin birth, even though my professors assure me that it most certainly is possible. I have been having doubts about some of the things they teach in creation science. I've seen some things on the internet that say the universe is billions of years old, with billions of galaxies out there that have billions of stars in them. It also says that our solar system is several billion years old. They talk about some other form of science that I never heard of before. They talk about telescopes that are up in space circling the earth studying this stuff. What are these telescopes? I never heard of such a thing. Where did all this come from? And they don't say anything about the earth being created in six days."

"Honey, I did the best job I could in trying to give you a good Christian education. These things up in space are idols, and the Bible forbids idol worship. Remember, the devil is very creative in leading people astray. You don't want to be wasting your precious time on the internet anyway. It will distract you from your studies to become a first lady. If you cannot become the first lady, at least you can become a first lady of one of our great corporations."

Lindsey did not get much comfort from her mother, and she didn't know what to think or do. She was extremely confused. Unknown to her, her mother was also beginning to have doubts. She was beginning to realize that literalism didn't provide satisfactory explanations for the nature of things. They parted, both with the uneasy feeling resulting from the emergence of doubt.

Next Chapter

Elena McPhee received a little extra funding as a result of some very creative accounting with NASA and the Mars Exploration Society. She used this financing diligently to gather and analyze phytoplankton data from around the world. What she found was cause for alarm. *Zooplanktus herbervorans* had increased its population exponentially upsetting the entire microbiome of the oceans. In addition the oceanic pH had reached a new low, but appeared to be leveling off. If this was the case, Alex would start to see an increase in atmospheric CO_2. Her concern was that the phytoplankton population was decreasing to dangerously low levels. She called for an immediate meeting with Alex.

"Alex, I have just sent you a detailed analysis of the oceanic biome and oceanic pH levels. If my analysis is correct, at some point, you should begin to detect changes in the atmosphere. *Zooplanktus herbervorans* has increased at an alarming rate, and I am afraid that it is reducing the phytoplankton population to dangerously low levels. You know what this means. Also, it appears that the oceanic pH, although low, appears to be leveling off. If so, you should start to detect a CO_2 increase in the atmosphere."

"Do you have any idea why the oceans started absorbing the atmospheric CO_2? I have been baffled by this. Up until about 2025, atmospheric CO_2 was increasing and then it leveled off."

"I think what might have happened is that with the unmentionable global warming, the oceans warmed more rapidly than the land or the atmosphere. This caused them to absorb more CO_2. It also moderated the temperature rise elsewhere. This set up a negative feedback loop that allowed our esteemed politicians to claim that global warming was a non issue. I think it is now coming to an end. I can't prove this, but it seems to make sense."

"I agree that it makes sense. You know that I was looking into the observations that gas mileage has been decreasing. As you know, I sent the report to the director on this in which I mentioned a few very unlikely explanations. I also raised your concerns in that report. I haven't heard a thing. O'Donnell has an iron grip not only on the Senate, but on the entire Congress and he requires that all reports have to go through his office. I think he buried it. I don't know what it will take to wake these bastards up. But temperatures may be rising again."

"I doubt that will wake them up. We have been in denial about this for decades."

"Is Socrates with you?"

"Yes, he is. Do you want to see him?"

"Let's go take him for a walk. A dog provides a relief from all the assholes we have to deal with. I am becoming convinced that dogs and other life forms have more intelligence than we do. In spite of our knowledge, we are the only species that systematically kills its own kind and destroys its habitat."

Next Chapter

O'Donnell was worried that all the attention paid to the virgin birth might result in part of the truth leaking out. To divert the public's attention, and because of his anger at McDonald, he put his plan into operation, which was to order Commerce to post the gas mileage report on TheTruth.gov. He also ordered them to post that piece of information that McDonald had inadvertently let slip that was stored deep within his medial temporal lobe. He told them to keep this activity strictly secret. He could do all of this because he was Senate majority leader and had great power; so great that his power could, if he wanted it to, challenge the president. But he decided that it was considerably more expedient to use his power in this subtler manner.[32]

NOAA Report to the Secretary of Commerce

Executive Summary

The Office of Oceanic and Atmospheric Research has been asked to address the issue of declining vehicular gas mileage. We assume this request was based on the hypothesis that atmospheric changes may be related to the reported decline. We know that the atmosphere has been warming, which results in less air density which should lead to an increase in gas mileage. However, this warming also increases the amount of water vapor in the air and the kinetic energy of air molecules, which would lead to a decrease in gas mileage. We examined these variables at observation sites located at mean sea level around the world and compared them to

---

[32] It occurred to O'Donnell that he might have to use climate change as a means to win elections now that he had lost the abortion issue, even though he thought this was total bullshit.

historical data. What we found, however, is that the main effect of increasing temperature is a significant increase in wind speed. Wind speed does have a directional component, usually west to east, but its impact on vehicle mileage is basically random, given that vehicles are traveling in all directions. Therefore, we did not find anything in the atmosphere that is causing decreased gas mileage.

However, as part of this study, we looked at historical and current data on atmospheric composition. This data was used to monitor the amount of CO_2 in the atmosphere. We found that this amount gradually increased over a number of decades, then increased sharply, but then leveled off. We know that the oceans capture much of the atmospheric CO_2, so we decided to test the hypothesis that this leveling off was a result of oceanic CO_2 capture. The dissolved CO_2 decreases oceanic pH.

Historical pH data from numerous monitoring stations around the world indicate that oceanic pH decreased gradually, then decreased dramatically before leveling off. These observations are very concerning. We have also observed ecological changes in the phytoplankton composition of the oceans. *Zooplanktus herbervorans* is a newly discovered organism that appears to have evolved very recently in response to the increasing oceanic acidity. We are monitoring it as best we can with limited funding, but it appears that it is consuming the phytoplankton. Phytoplankton are responsible for algae blooms, but they are essential in that they produce 50 percent of the world's oxygen. Our colleagues on the ISS have been reporting a decrease in observed algae blooms around the world. The earth is already losing its capacity to produce oxygen as a result of the loss of tropical rain forests. If fires increase while phytoplankton decrease, the probability of a positive feedback loop will increase to near certainty.

At the end of this report O'Donnell added the following: "President McDonald informed me that Environmental Resources, I assume with the assistance of Technology Systems International, has been hacking the computers in motor vehicles worldwide to cause them to gradually increase their gas consumption. This help explain ER's financial success."

TheTruth.gov had very little credibility with the press corps, but they did check it daily for indications of what the government might be up to. When they saw this posting, they were incredulous and immediately called the president's press secretary demanding a press conference. If the president refused, they would report the posting to news sources worldwide without delay.

James McMaster was unaware of this posting and requested a delay so that he could look into it. The press corps granted him a twenty-four-hour delay, and he logged into his computer. What he saw was shocking, so shocking that he went storming into the oval office. The president was not there, and he found him in his living quarters watching Weasel News.

"Mr. President, quick, come down to the Oval Office and log into TheTruth.gov. You have got to find out how this report got on there."

"What report? What are you talking about?"

"You will have to read it. I don't know where it came from."

McMaster realized that once McDonald read the posting, it would induce stress. He had the president read the report while he put in an emergency request for the services of Shirley Dumbaster. He had to make sure that she remained ignorant of the posting. If she became aware of it, in all probability, she would withdraw her services. And once the public became aware of it, all hell would break loose.
After McDonald finished reading the report his face turned red with anger.

"How did this shit get in here? Who the fuck authorized this?"

"We have only twenty-four hours to resolve this. If we don't come up with something, the press is going to report it. Holding them off for twenty-four hours was the best I could do."

"Goddamn it! Find out who did it."

"Mr. President, calm down. Shirley is here to help you." He escorted the president to his living quarters where Shirley was waiting.

Next Chapter

Lindsay returned to her dorm at AJBU in a state of extreme depression, and she started to cogitate about all the weird things that were happening to her.

I don't know what to think or believe, but I don't believe that I am pregnant by virtue of being a virgin. How can a virgin be pregnant? Mary was the only woman to have a virgin birth, but she was married to Joseph. I'm not married to anyone, and I don't have a boyfriend, and I never had sex. I didn't get any messages from an angel of the Lord. This just doesn't make any sense; it appears to actually be anti-biblical. And if it is anti-biblical, it can only mean that the devil did it. And if the devil did this to me, he probably also caused Nancy's death. What did I do to deserve this? If Mom gave me such a good Christian education, how could I possibly come under the influence of the devil?

She spent the next several hours trying to remember every aspect of her life from birth to the present in search of any flaws that could have caused her present state of despair. She didn't masturbate; in fact, she didn't know what masturbation was, so it is possible that she did it, but since she didn't know what it was, she couldn't have done it. She had NRA womb protection training. Wouldn't that have protected her? Eventually she became aware of dreams she had just as she was emerging into pubescence. She remembered these dreams being pleasurable and involving something that might be called sexual pleasure. But since she was naive about sex, she couldn't be sure. She was only more confused. And the intensity of this confusion was only making her more anxious.

Then she resorted to prayer. She didn't want to ask God for help because you are not supposed to ask God for favors. That would make you appear selfish, and being selfish is a sin. And sin is not good, and since it is not good, it will get you in trouble with God. And then you will have to ask for forgiveness. But what if God doesn't want to forgive you? All these thoughts just increased her anxiety. So all she could do was to repeat the Lord's Prayer over and over. This didn't relieve her anxiety, but at least it was not getting worse. Not now at least. Eventually all this repetition made her sleepy, and she lay down on her bed and took a nap.

It turned out that this nap was not restful. She had a dream, or was it a nightmare? She couldn't tell because she was asleep. It was a dream, or nightmare, about God. And God appeared to be very angry at her. When she awoke, she felt an extreme alienation from God. This only increased her anxiety and depression. She began to sweat—something that was very unladylike. And this increased her anxiety even more.

By this time, it was about midnight. She decided to go to the chapel and pray some more. She took her womb protector with her, even though now that she was pregnant, she would not need it. Not for that at least.

She prayed until 2:00 a.m., but her depression only got worse. It got so bad that she took her womb protector, and with no idea as to whether she would go to heaven or hell, she shot herself in the head.

Her doubt did not emerge fast enough.

Next Chapter

McMaster had no idea who could have published the report on TheTruth.gov. After considerable cogitation, he realized that TheTruth.gov was a website, and being a website, it involved computers, and since it involved computers, Technology Systems International might know something about it. He gave them a call.

When TSI received this call, they did not know what department to refer it to, but since it came from the government, and since national security liaison was the department most likely to have anything to do with the government, they sent it there. But national security liaison did not deal with the government directly. Their liaison was with National Security, which, despite its name, was a private corporation. Now NS had a TSI liaison department, and since the request came from TSI, it was sent there. It bounced back and forth between these liaison departments at each company.

Eventually, some lowly technician at one of these companies was able to trace the posting back to the Commerce Department. McMaster called Commerce and was put in touch with the secretary. The secretary had a vague recollection of having this report posted on TheTruth.gov and another vague recollection of O'Donnell ordering it to be kept secret. Now he was caught in a conflict between the legislative and executive branches of government. But Commerce was in the executive branch, and being in the executive branch, he had to do his executive duty, which was to tell the truth, the whole truth, and nothing but the truth. Which he did.

This was a very painful truth that initiated the arousal of intense agony within McMaster's psyche. How was he going to present this information to the president? They still had the press corps to deal with, and a press conference would certainly cause presidential anxiety. McMaster was unaware of the president's unusual medical condition, but strange behavior at press conferences was common, and controlling it required de-agitation services.

As he was pondering his dilemma, his secretary rushed in with the news of Lindsey Dense's suicide. After his initial shock, he realized that this might deflect the press's attention from the climate report.

Next Chapter

Doubts were starting to emerge in Martha's mind with increased intensity, which set up a conflict between her cerebral cortex and her amygdala. Then she received the news of Lindsey's suicide, which sent all her synapses into an electrochemical storm. She was overwhelmed with emotion. Her cerebral cortex could not function.

Mickey was at the Supreme Court hearing a complex case involving animal rights. He couldn't believe there was such a thing and was determined to make that perfectly clear. Then the bailiff interrupted the proceedings to bring him the news. He immediately called a recess and was escorted home in a state of shock.

As he entered, he was confronted by his wife. "How could God betray us like this? If this was a virgin birth, he would not let this happen. You gave her the gun and taught her to use it. What were you thinking? Don't we have too many guns in this country? Was she captured by the devil? What if the devil captures other people with guns? Are they all going to commit suicide or shoot one another? What's going to happen to the country? They were expecting a virgin birth. When they hear this, are they all going to become heathen? How can we put trust in God if that happens? God will be mad. He will make us take all references to him off our currency and out of our pledge." The amygdala was in full control.

Mickey, with all his legal expertise, was unable to apply it to his wife's queries. He could not think of anything in the Constitution that would apply. He even looked to natural law for answers, but that didn't work. Bad things happen in nature all the time. And he was dimly aware that they might be getting worse. He began to worry. *What if God cannot control nature?* It simply would not do to pursue this line of reasoning any further. It could lead to contradiction.

So he hugged his wife, took her hand, and said, "Let's pray." And they prayed. This brought comfort until Mickey realized that he had to plan a funeral and deal with the press. The latter would bring him embarrassment and indignity to the court. He won confirmation by the full expectation of a virgin birth.

Next Chapter

Before McMaster could report his findings to the president, he had an urgent message from Michael Dimpleberry at Weasel News about a press conference. This was very unusual. Weasel News had no interest in press conferences, so he thought it was about the suicide. He called Michael.

"Mike, Jim McMaster returning your call. What can I do for you?"

"Jim, we at Weasel just got the news from TheTruth.gov that the earth could be losing oxygen. The president has got to address this."

"Mike, he can't. He has to deal with the suicide. Isn't that much more newsworthy right now?"

"The newspapers are pressuring me to pressure you for a news conference. They say this oxygen thing is urgent and needs to be addressed immediately."

"What's the big deal? We got a suicide to deal with, a suicide that is going to upset the base. This is going to reflect very badly on the confirmation of Dense. We don't know how to deal with it. What if people start to think that he got her pregnant so that he could win confirmation? We're in a big pickle here."

"But you are going to be in a bigger pickle if you don't address the oxygen issue. We are talking about the possibility of wiping all life off the face of the planet. That's a much bigger issue than one suicide. You won't have a base when the masses become aware of this. Remember, we aren't making this up. It's on TheTruth.gov. That means it is the truth, the whole truth, and nothing but the truth. The government just said so. Calling it fake news won't work. Fake news can't exist on TheTruth. You yourself said so. McDonald had better come up with something to say and soon. If he doesn't, the press is going to report it, and this includes Weasel. It's on TheTruth, so we have to cover it."

At this point, the job of press secretary was becoming very unenjoyable. In fact, it was pure torture. He knew the president couldn't address the oxygen issue. He wasn't sure if the president knew what oxygen was. He would have to persuade the president to do a press conference on the suicide and hope that this would satisfy them. And he had no idea what the president would do when he told him O'Donnell had posted the report.

Next Chapter

When the news that Alexander's report was on TheTruth.gov reached NOAA, the director issued an edict telling the entire agency to a take vacation. He was afraid that the agency might be discovered by the administration, and he didn't want the agency to receive the heat of presidential anger. Nor did he want it to lose funding. When Alex received the edict, he called Elena into his office.

"Sweetie, someone posted the report I wrote on TheTruth, and the director has ordered the entire agency to go on vacation. When the shit hits the fan, he wants everyone out of here. He is afraid that the administration will discover us and wipe us out. I have been thinking that we need to get away anyway. I know a place high in the mountains of Montana that I would like to take you to. It is a great place to hike, and Socrates will love it."

What Alex did not say was that the data he had been analyzing was telling him the earth was in a precarious situation. The phytoplankton in the oceans had been wiped out, so oxygen was no longer coming from that source. If there were extensive forest fires, the oxygen level would dip below the level at which humans could function. Behavior would become erratic, and since the president already had erratic behavior, his actions would be unpredictable. He could go ballistic and start launching nuclear weapons. He also thought that, since CO_2 is heavier than air, what oxygen remained might be displaced to higher elevations. This may have been wishful thinking.

They left the office and began packing. It would take two and a half days to get all the way out to the Beartooth Range in south central Montana. They would drive to Red Lodge and from there to the trailhead to Mystic Lake. They would hike to the lake, and stay in a cozy rustic cabin. There was an extensive trail system in the area for hiking. He was looking forward to the Stillwater Trail in particular. He also was bothered by what his report had predicted.

Next Chapter

Jim McMaster called the president's secretary to see if he was back in the Oval Office. He was, so it was time to approach this delicate matter. He hoped that Shirley had done a vigorous job of presidential de-agitation. If she had, the president might be so relaxed that he could discuss the idea of a press conference on the suicide and hope the president might not remember the posting on TheTruth.gov. He was taking a big chance here because he knew the press would bring up the posting. But they were going to report it anyway so this was the best he could do.

"Mr. President, the country is mourning the suicide of Lindsey Dense. Not that they care about Lindsey, because they don't. But they sure care about her fetus. You need to use your very best rhetorical skills to put them at ease. I know you can do this. Look how you rouse people up at your rallies. They go bonkers over you. I'll do everything I can to help you. I will make sure you have Shirley's services both before and after the press conference. All you have to do is appear very, very mournful. If you could possibly shed a tear, that would be great. If Shirley gets you relaxed enough right before the conference, you just might be able to do it. This time you might want to use the teleprompter. You definitely won't want to go off script. I suggest you do some serious rehearsals. But do them now. This can't wait. It has to be done tomorrow."

McMaster was hoping all this planning would keep the president's mind completely off the TheTruth thing. He called the technical staff to arrange for a teleprompter and a speechwriter to compose a script.

Next Chapter

Polly Burman and Eugene Furman were circling comfortably in a meditative state, watching the earth float by beneath them. They didn't have much to do because serious science had been discontinued nationwide, which included the ISS, even though it was not technically in the nation, but above it, sometimes, depending on its orbit. For some time they had been observing the fires in the Amazon each time they passed over it. These observations spoiled their meditative state, but they learned to recover once the desolation was no longer visible. They had already reported the decline in algae blooms and were aware of the fact that the phytoplankton had been consumed by *Zooplanktus herbervorans*.

Since they were bored, they decided to do their own experiment by having sex in space. Although they were nimble and flexible from their yoga training, they were weightless. Floating around in a weightless state made things difficult. They tried strapping themselves down, but that proved impractical. It made maneuverability difficult. So they got undressed and stashed their clothes so they would not get in the way. They held on to each other, and Eugene stuck his member deep inside Polly's. But once he started pumping, things got out of hand. Pumping while being weightless caused them to float about in very close quarters, which caused them to bump into the walls of the ISS. Not only do the walls of the ISS have no bump protection, but they have all sorts of objects sticking out of them. Some of these are for scientific purposes, now rendered useless from the lack of scientific interest. Others are for safety and emergency purposes. And still others are for communication. And the rest are various computers for different purposes. People bumping into these things, even though weightless, can get bruised. That is because pumping is a force that, according to Newton's second law of motion[33], causes a mass to accelerate, and an accelerating mass in a container is going to impact the walls of that container. The ISS was a highly sophisticated container, and when you bump into the walls of such a container the walls exert an opposing force upon the object bumping into them. This sends that object off in the opposite direction until it bumps into the opposite wall. The object just keeps bumping back and forth. Since these particular walls had sharp objects sticking out of them, Polly and Eugene were starting to lose interest in their experiment.

But before they lost total interest in their experiment the ISS approached the zenith of its orbit over northern Canada. At that moment, while Polly and Eugene were still entangled, they were moving toward a window and saw a humongous flare over the entire arctic region. This caused a rapid detanglement, and they floated back to where their clothes were stashed. They could not report this observation back to NASA while naked.

Polly exclaimed, "What do you think that was? It looked like an explosion."

"I don't know, but I have a theory. You know all that methane that is stored in the permafrost. And all that methane Environmental Resources has been pumping back into the ground. And all that drilling they are doing throughout the arctic. And all that fracking. And the unmentionable climate change. Well, what I think happened is that the earth simply farted one huge fart of methane, and with all that drilling, there was probably a fair amount of welding going on, and that welding caused the methane to explode. When we pass by again, I expect that we will see fires in the boreal forest, and all

---

[33] $F = ma$

those spruce bogs have more methane that will set up a positive reinforcement loop."

"Holy shit. That will consume the remaining oxygen."

"I know. I'm calling ground control right now."

Next Chapter

Instead of engaging in his late-night activities on the internet and enjoying the arousal they provided, McDonald had to prepare for the morning news conference. As a result, he was agitated, but, as promised by his press secretary, this agitation was relieved right before he had to face the press. He entered the Rose Garden and stepped up to the podium.

"Members of the press and everyone else: let us have a moment of silence for the fetus of Lindsey Dense, but not Lindsey Dense herself. Her murderous act deprived the nation of a virgin birth. I can think of no crime more treacherous, despicable, and unconscionable than that. This will deprive America of its virility, and I promised to 'Make America Virile Again,' and now that I have been deprived of the opportunity to make America virile again, her act was clearly an act of treason. I will not stand for treason or reason. I will not! I will not!"

McMaster went into a state of severe apprehension. The president was going way off script.[34] He was not consoling the nation but trying to get it riled up. If he got it riled up enough there might be violence. And right, now with the financial crisis and the nation in an uproar over abortion and people trying to get out who couldn't get out because Canada erected a wall, there already was too much violence.

The president continued, "I know Lindsey Dense was the daughter of our esteemed chief justice and our esteemed chief justice is a man of the highest moral character. Such a

---

[34] The reason McDonald kept going off script was that he could not read. He disguised this inability through bombast and the use of voice to text software. No one was aware of this fact.

man could not have raised a devious daughter. So, somehow, the daughter got corrupted. And that corruption could have come from only one source, the opposition party. That means that the opposition party is a party of treason and reason. When we are finished here, I am going to order a congressional investigation into the opposition party.[35] We will be virile again."

Lost was the moment of silence.

"Even though I have absolutely no desire to take your questions, I have been advised that I must do so."

"Mr. President, Michael Dimpleberry of Weasel News. I know this question is going to come up, and since I am on friendly terms with your administration, and since you are more likely to trust me than the other members of the press corps, and since we admire your administration, and what I am about to bring up certainly must not be true, but the fact that it is on TheTruth.gov means I am forced to bring it up even though I don't want to. My apologies, Mr. President. There is a report on TheTruth.gov that says the world might be running out of oxygen. Since this could not possibly be true, but since it is on TheTruth, we need you to explain. Again, my apologies Mr. President."

"Michael, the world cannot be running out of oxygen, whatever that is, but if it is, we can get Environmental Resources to get more of it."

This response may or may not have satisfied Michael Dimpleberry and the crew at Weasel News, but it put the rest of the press corps into an uproar. There was intense competition for recognition. Eventually Paul Rudd of the *NYT&F* prevailed.

"Mr. President, it also says on TheTruth.gov that Environmental Resources has been hacking motor vehicle

---

[35] Exactly how such an investigation would work when the opposition party was a part of Congress was unclear.

computers worldwide to cause them to consume more gas. And, as you know, gas consumption creates more CO_2, and as you also know the O_2 part of CO_2 is oxygen. So if Environmental Resources is consuming oxygen, how are they going to make more of it?"

This was a very stress producing question for the president which started to set up a positive feedback loop. Since he didn't know what they were talking about, except for an emerging recollection of some bullshit showing up on TheTruth.gov, an erection started to form. He started to squirm and wiggle around.

At this moment Paul Rudd received a message from the New York office.

"Mr. President, I just received a report that NASA said there was a methane explosion all over the arctic and that this explosion has caused mammoth forest fires in the boreal forest. The report on TheTruth says that the phytoplankton in the oceans have died off, so this means the world may be running out of oxygen right now.[36] What are you going to do about this?"

This did it. The squirming and wiggling became intense. He started to grab his crotch in anguish. He was sweating. His tie came undone. His press secretary rushed to his aid.

Now Shirley Dumbaster was nearby in the White House to service the president after the news conference, and she heard everything. She was suddenly pissed off, so pissed off that she came running out and gave a detailed report on all the services she had provided to the president on behalf of Environmental Resources. Now there was total pandemonium, and all hell broke loose, not just in the Rose Garden, but

---

[36] The air was about 20 percent oxygen. When that percentage falls to 16 percent human function is impaired. At 6 percent death occurs.

everywhere because news spreads from its source around the world almost instantaneously.

The president made a hasty retreat into the White House up to his living quarters and locked the door. Before the oxygen depletion reached dangerous levels, the people heard that the president had bled to death from a penile rupture. The whereabouts of O'Donnell were unknown.

The chief justice was in his chambers watching the press conference. He rushed home just before all hell broke loose. Martha had been watching the press conference at home, and now, at long last, the emergence of her doubt was complete.

When the chief justice entered the house, she shouted at him.

"Get out of here. I want to die in this house alone. You contributed to this mess. How could I have been so stupid? Why couldn't I have seen through all your fetal bullshit? Now our daughter is dead, and we are all going to be dead. When you were vice president all you did was praise that goddamn Environmental Resources. Now look what happened."

"But Martha, all I was doing was trying to protect the sanctity of the unborn."

"Don't you realize that, for you, the sanctity of the unborn means that the unborn will remain forever unborn?"

Mickey Dense had no answer. Legal training had not prepared him for this. Martha's suffering, along with everyone else's suffering, was soon relieved.

Next Chapter

Elena and Alex had a pleasant hike up to their cozy, rustic cabin on Mystic Lake. Alex had been here before for a field trip that was part of a geology course he'd taken at Amherst. He loved the area and wanted to share its beauty with Elena. The cabin was well stocked with food, marrow bones for Socrates, and various high-caliber spirits. It had very comfortable beds, a small but functional kitchen, and a porch with chairs suitable for relaxing with a very nice view of the lake. When at the cabin, they spent most of their time on the porch. They were sitting there now, enjoying the view while imbibing world-class Kentucky bourbon.

"Alex, I know why you brought me here. It's because we don't have much time, isn't it?"

"Sweetie, you know the data as well as I do. I thought we might survive a little longer up here. CO_2 is heavier than air, and I'm hoping it will sink into low-lying areas, particularly Washington, DC, before it replaces the air up here. This is a pure guess, but we can hope."

"It's not a lot to hope for, but I appreciate your effort to make the end as pleasant as possible. What do you think was the biggest reason for our failure? Not you and I, but our failure as a species."

"That's a good question. One obvious reason is that we failed at governance. We never made a serious effort to solve the problem of governance, which is much different than politics, and as a result, we ended up with certified tail wagging-horses' asses in positions of power. And this happened worldwide. We never developed a genuine democracy anywhere. It was all a lot of rhetoric that promoted the interests of corporations."

"How do you think that came about?"

"I never studied economics, but I remember hearing that Adam Smith had this idea that the pursuit of private interest promoted the public interest. And this idea was used to justify the idea of unregulated markets. Well, obviously, that is pure unadulterated bullshit. It gave corporate power carte blanche, and here we are."

"Do you think these horses' asses were ever happy? Did they ever experience joy? Appreciate beauty?"

"I think they were spiritually void. They had no inner life. They were always outwardly directed, but vacuous on the inside. In other words, miserable, and all they could do was to inflict their misery on the rest of the world. And they used religion for political purposes to do it. They may have been intelligent, but they had no wisdom. The Native Americans were not advanced scientifically, but they had wisdom. They knew that everything they depended on, including themselves, came from nature. So they had a certain reverence for nature. For us, nature was a thing to be exploited. That was pure hubris, and here we are."

"This is really good bourbon. How could a state like Kentucky that gave us O'Donnell produce such good bourbon? It's a shame, isn't it?"

"You would have thought that the good bourbon would have made O'Donnell more mellow. You would have thought that, if anything, it would have given him a bit of a spiritual life. If anything, it did the opposite, and here we are."

"When you look at all this beauty around us, it's hard to believe that it is all going to be lost. It looks strong and majestic, but it is really fragile. The loss of one element can bring the whole biological edifice crashing down."

"It's very fragile; we destroyed it, and here we are."

While Elena and Alex were enjoying the view and the spirits, they got a call from the director of NOAA. The director was not in Washington, but he'd gotten a call from NASA that confirmed everything in Alex's report. He advised them to just stay where they were because there was nothing that could be done. No amount of money, political power, military power, technology, economic growth, religious faith, competition, cooperation, wisdom, or anything else was going to solve this problem. Oxygen was the only thing that could solve it. Some people thought they could save themselves by stealing oxygen tanks from hospitals and other sources, but more often than not, they ended up incinerating themselves.

Alex explained that he came to the mountains with the hope that what little oxygen remained might be displaced by the CO_2 to higher elevations. The director thought that this might possibly buy them a little time, but that would be all. As they were having this conversation, Alex noticed that the sky was becoming darker from the fires in Canada. He said goodbye to the director and wished him luck. The director did the same.

Elena and Alex, being rational people, did what any rational person would do in this situation, and that was to make love. But before they did this, they made sure Socrates had food and water. Because of his lower body mass, he might require less oxygen and survive a bit longer. All of them eventually succumbed as the fires consumed the remaining oxygen. And there they were.

Last (Final) Chapter

The earth fart that Polly and Eugene reported to ground control set off mass hysteria, so communication was lost. They found it difficult to enter into a meditative state. They just watched the fires below.

"Gene, do you think anyone bothered to contact Wyzinsky and his crew? They will not want to come back."

"That's a good question. I doubt it since we can't establish contact, and we have no way of contacting them. I hope they realize that with lost communication something is drastically wrong."

Both Polly and Eugene were in a state of shock. They were observing the whole picture. Fires burning that were darkening the earth in a thick layer of smoke. For a very long time, they had nothing to say to each other. They were in a state of suspended animation, which was not the same as a meditative state. Shock can stop all mental processes, which is different than meditation. Meditation requires intense discipline to enter a thoughtless state. So they just floated around doing and thinking nothing.

Since the ISS was stocked with food and water and could generate its own oxygen for several months from the resources on board, Polly and Eugene survived longer than their fellow beings below. After their lengthy period of shock, they started to reflect on what had gone wrong—very, very wrong.

"Polly, how did we get into this mess?"

"I didn't take any political science courses when we were at MIT, but I think it is obvious that Congress abdicated all its powers to the executive and became the dog that got wagged by its tail. Totally useless. Just a loud mouthpiece for the president. And when the president is nothing but an asshole, you have broken government. And the people were powerless to change it. And here we are."

"That's all true, but I think the corporations were at fault also. They managed to capture the political process for their own benefit. Just look at all the damage those fucking mining companies did all over the world. And after the consolidation, Environmental Resources just went wild extracting everything, and Entertainment and Distractions managed to keep the vast majority in the dark. And here we are."[37]

"And recycling was a joke. It made people feel good that they were saving the environment, but that, too, kept them in the dark. And here we are."

"Do you think anything could have been done?"

"Not at this late stage. But do you remember hearing about the OPEC thing in the 1970s? That produced artificial gas shortages in the U.S. They lowered speed limits to conserve fuel. What they should have done was initiate a mammoth government program to develop alternative sources of energy. And conservation, not consumption, should have been the economic goal. I don't know how you would have done that, but it should have been attempted. Now the earth is burning, and here we are."

"You mentioned Congress being a big problem? How could we have fixed it?"

"Elections were a joke. Everything was gerrymandered, and the parties controlled everything, and there wasn't much difference between them. It seems that the people in politics had more tongue than brains. They got ego satisfaction by wagging their tongues. If they jolted their brains, maybe they could have come up with some solutions. But those solutions would have had to have been initiated a long, long time ago. And here we are."

"What do you think a genuine leader would have done?"

---

[37] They did not know about the hacking of motor vehicle computers.

"A real leader would have used our common citizenship as a means of uniting the country. Instead they abused the idea by focusing on immigration and using it as a means of division. And here we are."

And there they were, on board the ISS for several more weeks. Eventually supplies ran out, and oxygen was depleted, and they joined their fellow beings below in a permanent state of extinction where the unborn would remain forever unborn and the universe, on the basis of what was known about it, lost its consciousness.

When assholes rule
Shit happens.

Epilogue

This we know: the earth does not belong to man, man belongs to the earth. All things are connected like the blood that unites us all. Man did not weave the web of life; he is merely a strand in it. Whatever he does to the web, he does to himself.

—Chief Seattle

As the embers faded away, and morning merged into night, equality was achieved,

and the end of history had arrived, for this was the last day, and darkness fell upon the deep.

Appendix

The following paper was presented to the Theoretical Physical Sociology Subgroup of the Sociology Section of the International Social Science Society's Annual Conference held on January 27-31, 2020 at Stanford University, San Francisco, CA.

The Theory of Sociothermodynamics
Dr. Michelle Stanley, BS, MSSc, PhD

> *The present biological spasm of the human species— for spasm it is—is bound to have an impact on our future political organization. The shooting wars and the political upheavals that have studded the globe with an appalling frequency during recent history are only the first political symptoms of this spasm.*
>
> ...
>
> *The end of the social conflict implies a radical change in man's nature, nay, his biological nature.*
>
> ...
>
> *To observe that social conflict is an outgrowth of the struggle of man with his environment is to recognize a fairly obvious fact, but not to explain it.*
>
> Nicholas Georgescu-Roegen, *The Entropy Law and the Economic Process*, pp. 306-7, Harvard University Press, Cambridge MA 1971, 1999.

Sociothermodynamics is an emerging sub-discipline within theoretical physical sociology. Here, we examine the hypotheses of sociothermodynamics and explore the variables that are needed to compute the dependent variable of sociothermodynamics—social entropy. In explicating the nature of these hypotheses and their underlying variables, we hope that the knowledge so gained may be applied to mitigating their predicted adverse consequences. Sociothermodynamics, at this stage of its development, is a theoretical extension of thermodynamics. Thus, it is used to describe a dissipative process through which societies experience increasing social disorder, which ultimately results in social death in the form of heat. Heat and time are interrelated phenomena that are unidirectional and irreversible. Our hope is that by understanding this process, we can extend the time variable so that social death will co-incide with the inevitable heat death of our fair planet.

The Hypotheses of Sociothermodynamics

First Hypothesis

Social forces increase with increasing population. There are two social forces: the conservative force and the liberal force. The conservative force is bidirectional. The liberal force is unidirectional and orthogonal to the conservative force. Over time, the conservative force tends to overwhelm the liberal force unless ethical work is injected into the system, but ethical work has a tendency to transform into unethical work and useless work. Figure 1 is an illustration.

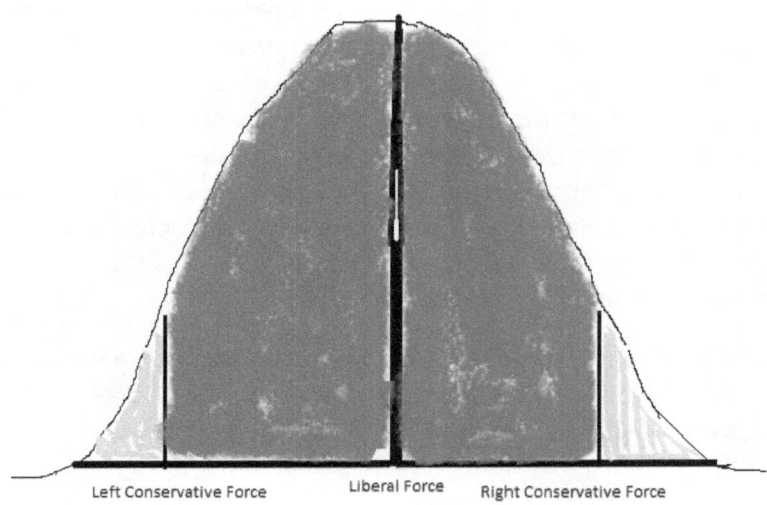

Left Conservative Force   Liberal Force   Right Conservative Force

Figure 1
Taylor, Ed; *A Nonnormal Use of the Normal Distribution*,
Icelandic Journal of Physical Sociology, No. 55 Vol. 2, pp. 3-
15

Second Hypothesis

There is a tendency for social entropy to increase over time.
This is a direct result of the bidirectionality of the conservative
force and the tendency for ethical work to degrade into
unethical and useless work. There are many variables that
contribute to social entropy (SE).

Third Hypothesis

Ultimately the social entropy ends up as heat that spreads
throughout the system.

Variables

Before we consider the sociothermodynamic variables, we
need to discuss social forces, which are illustrated in Figure 1.
The conservative force has a left and a right component which
correspond to the left and right portions of the curve. The left
conservative force exhibits a tendency toward governmental
social control. China is the most obvious current example. The

123

right conservative force exhibits a tendency toward corporate social control. This often is not as obvious because, on the surface, it appears that government is involved. But whereas, in the case of the left force, government exerts complete control over the means of production, in the case of the right force, corporations control not only the means of production, but the government itself. Today, the vast majority of societies are right-force dominated. The social characteristic of the conservative force is extreme hierarchy.

The liberal social force tends toward a non hierarchal social system where social control is diffuse—i.e., social control is the result of shared social norms. Social democracy is the best example of such a system.

Variables That Affect Social Entropy:

Work

This is the main variable involved in social entropy. In sociothermodynamics work must be performed by institutions within the society to transfer energy into the society which is used to promote social stability. However this is complicated by the fact that work can take several forms. Ethical work is that form which promotes social stability. But there is also unethical work which degrades social stability, and useless work that is relatively neutral. For our purposes, we will use net ethical work which is defined as:

$$W = \int_{i=1}^{i=n} I dC$$

where i = number of social institutions

I = institutional integrity

and dC = institutional complexity

The institutional integrity factor allows us to control for unethical work, and, for the most part, we can ignore useless work.

Externalities (E)

Externalities are those things that are not factored into the costs of production but happen to have social costs, which occasionally can be extreme. On rare occasions, an externality may have a positive effect. Pollution is the most common example of an externality that inflicts costs upon society, but the corporation producing it gets a free ride. These externalities accumulate over time, contributing to an increase in social entropy.

Resource Leakage (RL)

It is impossible to use any resource with 100 percent efficiency; there is always some leakage into the environment. An obvious example is energy, where a relatively small percentage ends up in the form of useful work. But there is waste all along the production process, and none of this waste is factored into the costs of production.

Biomass Reduction (BR)

Biomass reduction is the loss of biomass planet-wide. To the uninitiated, it may appear that the increasing human population would increase biomass, but, in fact, human activity is taking a severe toll on total biomass. Entire populations are being reduced and wiped out in some locations, and many species are going extinct. While war has a tendency to decrease the human population, it is counteracted by the propensity to copulate. However, it does increase environmental destruction and species loss.

The following formula is a sub-hypothesis within the second hypothesis of our theory, which says that the total biomass of the earth will decline as the human biomass increases:

$$BR_t = (BM_h e^{at} + BM_i e^{(\frac{1}{b})t})$$

where BR_t = biomass reduction at time t

BM_h = human biomass

BM_i = initial biomass

a = growth rate of human biomass

b = decay rate of total biomass

If we assume a growth rate of 3.5 percent for the human population and a decay rate of 5 percent for the total biomass of the earth, we find that the total biomass remaining after fifty years is 45.492 GtC from an initial biomass of 500 GtC. This reduction will be standardized as a percentage ratio.

Racism (R)

Racism is endemic in most societies except where there is complete homogeneity. The fact that racism is totally irrational, but prevalent makes it a major contributor to social discord, which obviously increases social entropy. The index of racism is defined as:

$$R = \sum_s \binom{n}{1} \sum_{g=1}^{n} (CE * g)$$

where CE = coefficient of exclusion

g = number of groups in a given society

s = number of societies

Inequality (I)

While complete equality is not attainable, inequality beyond its natural level is undesirable. Basic differences in our biological makeup (which has nothing to do with race) guarantee a base line level of inequality. Also, if we were all the same, there would be no adaptability in the population. However, extreme inequality is destructive of the social order. We will use the Gini coefficient as our index of inequality.

Unintended Consequences (UC)

Public policy produces many unintended consequences that are often in direct opposition to the intended result. The prime example is the war on drugs which has created violent criminal syndicates that are paragons of capitalist production. Not only are they efficient, but they have the added advantage that their product, and thus their income, is tax free. Thus, they can out compete any corporation that has state sanction through their higher return on investment. This is a very difficult variable to measure. In each society, it will be necessary to obtain a random sample of policies that have been enacted and count the number of unanticipated consequences they have generated and then standardize this number into an index.

Technology (T)

One would expect a high level of technological development to be inversely related to social entropy. However, technology can lead to economic power being concentrated in the hands of technological geniuses. It was thought, particularly with the emergence of the internet, that technology would have a democratizing effect, but as we have seen with the social network, it has created social discord. To measure this variable, we will need to create a score for each society that indicates the net positivity or negativity of its technological development.

Corruption (C)

Corruption ranges from petty bribery to organized crime. Unfortunately, it is common in most social systems. It becomes particularly dangerous when it infects governmental functions. Corporate entities operating under the law of laissez-faire have a tendency to engage in corrupt practices unless regulated by government. But when government becomes corrupt, the entire society becomes corrupt. There are several indices currently available. These will need to be improved and extended so that they cover more societies.

Social Friction (F)

Societies range along a continuum from the highly cooperative to the most competitive. Cooperative societies have a relatively low index of social friction and are located within the dark area of Figure 1. Competitive societies have a high index of social friction and fall within the light area. These societies are much more numerous than the low-friction societies. Friction is also directly transformed into heat and is very difficult to measure for entire societies. We propose measuring the amount and magnitude of political rhetoric in each society during the six-month period prior to a major election. This number can then be standardized into a political pomposity index, which will serve as a proxy for social friction. From a thermodynamic perspective, it should be noted that the energy put into political campaigns rapidly ends up as useless heat.

Political Pressure (PP)

Political pressure is an elusive concept that is somewhat counterintuitive. The dark area in Figure 1 represents the diffuse political pressure of non-hierarchical societies, whereas the light areas represent extreme hierarchy. Thus, as the area under the curve decreases and is squished into the tails, the political pressure increases.

Political pressure is defined as:

$$\int_a^b f(PP)dpp$$

This function is used to compute the area under the tails of the normal distribution. Political pressure will increase (i.e., the area under the curve decreases) until it reaches a critical pressure point. This point is known as the Georgescu-Roegen point of biological spasticity. At that point, the society experiences a biological spasm and explodes, resulting in a rapid increase of social entropy. If this happens in insignificant societies (sometimes referred to as "shithole[38] societies"), it will not threaten the world order. But if it happens in a major society or several societies simultaneously, the world-wide consequences will be catastrophic. Currently there are various indices that are used to measure the authoritarianism of various societies. Again, we propose improving these measures, extending them to more societies and using the standardized index as a proxy for political pressure.

Asshole[39] Index (AHI)

---

[38] This term is common in the vernacular, but it has recently entered the revised official presidential lexicon. Normally it is used as a noun, but here its function is adjectival and refers to societies of a certain type. The lexicographers have not provided any documentation on this adjectival use. As a noun, the meaning is ambiguous. Does it refer to an orifice through which excrement is expelled or does it refer to the opening of a receptacle into which excrement is deposited? This receptacle may be as simple as a hole dug in the ground or as elaborate as the gold plated apparatus available to the president. As an adjective, it appears to refer to societies that have been colonized, imperialized, and pulverized by Western capitalistic exploitation. They were initially used as a source of natural resources and slaves. When they no longer served this purpose (as a result of resource exhaustion) they were used as a sink for the toxic waste and detritus of capitalism. This excremental function may explain the emergence of the term into the presidential lexicon.

[39] This is a common term in the vernacular. (The technical term is *proctopore*, which is not in common use, so we will employ the vernacular.) It is a noun. We assume that it has entered the revised official presidential

This is a proposed index that will be used to indicate the level of moral degeneracy in a society. It will be difficult to measure because consideration must be paid to both the number of assholes in a given society and their locus. If they are located in high corporate or governmental positions, they can be extremely dangerous. If minimally dispersed in the lower levels of society, but absent from positions of power, their effect is more of a nuisance that results in wasted resources. *Merriam-Webster* defines *asshole* as "a stupid, annoying, or detestable person." We may have to use the level of stupidity in a given society as a proxy for this index, since this is at least theoretically measurable at the societal level.

Formal Statement of the Hypotheses

First Hypothesis

$$F_l + 2F_c = f(P)$$

For our purposes, this is an increasing function.

Second Hypothesis:

---

lexicon, but we don't know if it has been sanctioned for public use. We have no recollection of its appearance in the main-stream media. This could be the result of political correctness, which is still deeply embedded in some of our social institutions. The hole in this term refers to an anatomical orifice, but it also has a direct relationship to the hole in the term *shithole*. The material excreted from the hole of the asshole is usually, but not necessarily always, deposited directly into the hole of the shithole,. This anatomical use is clear. But the term also is used in reference to a particular type of individual. This meaning is widely shared and understood, but it is difficult to define. It falls in the category of you know one when you see one. It is this second meaning that is employed here.

$$SE = \sum_{s=1}^{s=n} W - (E + RL + BR + R + I + UC$$
$$+ T + C + F + PP + AHI)$$

where s = the number of societies.

Third Hypothesis

$$sE \rightarrow \varphi$$

where φ is dissipated heat.

Multicollinearity

The astute reader will notice that we have a rather severe problem with these variables since a number of them share the property of multicollinearity. Specifically, there is a relatively high correlation between racism and inequality. Likewise, there is a relatively high correlation between corruption and the asshole index, and these variables share lesser correlations with social friction, political pressure, and technology. To correct for this problem, we propose using systematic complex multivariate combinatorics to create a single variable adjusted with appropriate weights. The second hypothesis is now stated as:

$$\sum_{s=1}^{s=n} W - (E + RL + BR + UC + MV_c)$$

where MV_c = our multivariate transformation to a single variable.

Discussion

Although our proposal to test this theory in practice may lead to accusations of physics envy, the fact is that those accusations have already been leveled at economics, and that discipline is highly regarded. We are not unaware of the difficulty involved in measuring these variables, but all scientific disciplines originated with difficult measurement problems. The ingenuity involved in solving these problems has resulted in our highest intellectual advancement. We aim at no less.

Conclusion

The purpose of theoretical physical sociology is to illuminate the natural processes that underlie the evolution of societies, human society in particular. It may be considered an extension of sociobiology. Sociothermodynamics is of special interest because once it is fully developed, it will provide the means to allow us to radically slow down the societal entropic process. Hopefully the National Science Foundation, in its quest for scientific excellence through its ethical work, will invest some of its resources in developing the measurement techniques and collecting the data that will test these hypotheses and raise their status to that of scientific laws of nature. The theory of sociothermodynamics predicts that we are on a path leading toward a biological spasm that may eradicate life on this planet unless drastic measures are taken. We know that the social entropic process is irreversible, but we have the ability to drastically slow it down.

Partial Transcript of the Panel Discussion of the Theoretical Physical Sociology Subgroup of the Sociology Section of the International Social Science Society's Annual Conference

Dr. Ralph Arrowhead (RA), moderator:

"Our panelists today consist of Dr. Michelle Stanley, the esteemed author who presented her theory of sociothermodynamics this morning, Dr. Clorissa Panderhook, a physical sociologist from the Axewold Institute of Citizenship and Public Affairs in Syracuse, New York, and Dr. Mohammed el Plasio, a physicist who has a joint appointment with the physics department at the University of Minnesota and the University's Humpback Institute of Public Affairs. We will begin with Dr. Panderhook."

Dr. Panderhook (CP):

"Dr. Stanley has presented us with a challenging theory in theoretical physical sociology, which is an emerging discipline that is just beginning to build its intellectual foundation. Her work will contribute greatly to the strength of that foundation. My purpose today is to critique her work to help elucidate its methodology. She has rightfully raised the problem of multicollinearity. She has introduced a number of variables and suggested that they be standardized as indices that give the impression that they have a common unit of measurement. This is highly problematic in itself, but in addition, it appears that they each have the same weight. How do you propose to handle the relative importance of their contribution to social entropy? In addition, I believe their relative importance (if this is the right word) will vary from society to society. How do you propose taking this into account?

"Your theory implies that the sociothermodynamic process follows a smooth, continuous curve. In addition to multicollinearity, I think there will be many feedback loops among these variables that will radically alter how the process behaves and make it much more difficult to predict future events. Again, the process will vary from society to society.

"In addition, I think you will have a difficult time measuring the level of stupidity in societies. This is culturally relative. I think it would be easier to use some graduate students who are as ideologically neutral as possible to simply count the number of assholes in high places in each society and weight this number by the total population of each society. They can do this through the scrutiny of news media that has worldwide coverage. It is impossible to count the total number in any given society.

"This is a minor point, but I think racism, although a major social problem, is too narrow. There can be forms of exclusion that are not necessarily racist—misogyny, for example. I think what you mean is exclusion, so why not just use the coefficient of exclusion? If this doesn't work, then use it to compute an exclusion index."

RA: "Thank you, Dr. Panderhook. I am sure your comments will be well received. Now, Dr. el Plasio."

Dr. Mohammed el Plasio (MeP):

"Let me explain my presence here. I hold a dual appointment because there is a serious concern within the physics community that our best students, after years of study, are applying their talents to such fields as finance, economics, and computer science. While the latter has a somewhat logical connection to physics, the first two do not and are draining our discipline of its future practitioners. You mentioned "physics envy." This is no laughing matter. So I have been charged with investigating what it is about the squishy social sciences that is so attractive to our students. For the life of me, after attending this conference and my observations at the Humpback Institute, I cannot understand why a student trained in the hard disciplines would waste his or her talents in the social sciences. Yes, economics has, what appears on paper at least, pseudo-sophisticated mathematical theories. But these bear no relation to reality, as is well known, even in the social sciences.

"Thermodynamics is a serious discipline within physics and chemistry. Applying it to sociology is sheer nonsense. If we are to solve the serious problems that you raise, we need more people trained in the hard sciences. I thank the moderator for this opportunity to express my opinion."

RA: "Dr. Stanley, do you wish to respond?"

Dr. Michelle Stanley (MS):

"Thank you, Dr. Arrowhead. In response to Dr. el Plasio, I can only say that throughout history, every science was born of a science that preceded it with perhaps the exception of mathematics. I realize that physics is a bedrock science and that we need more physicists. I have no idea why students of physics are attracted to the social sciences. They must find economic theory exciting or the monetary rewards of finance enticing
　　　"In reply to Dr. Panderhook, her comments are well taken. The purpose of my paper was to start to lay the foundation for a theory of sociothermodynamics. The methodological problems are immense, which is why I hope that we can, yes, attract more people to this sub-discipline, but also secure funding to gather data and refine it to rigorously test our hypotheses."

The panel discussion continued for some time debating arcane aspects of the sociolthermodynamic theory.

RA: "I will now open the discussion to members of the audience. There are microphones in the aisles."

Member of the Audience (MA_x)

MA_1: "Dr. Stanley, do you really think the loss of biomass is going to be so drastic?"

MS: "Yes, I do. Much of what is being lost is not obvious. Insect populations, for example, are declining rapidly. We have no idea what pollution may be doing to the micro-environment inhabited by bacteria, protozoa, and archaea. Pollution of the oceans is a serious matter. If we lose the phytoplankton in the oceans, this will disrupt the entire aquatic food chain. The sonic testing that the navy is conducting is driving the mammals of the ocean nuts. Then, if you factor in deforestation and other such stupidities, the loss of biomass is extreme. And, as Dr. Panderhook pointed out, there may be feedback loops that accelerate the process."

MA₂: "Dr. Stanley, as I remember, your father was interested in the problem of technicism. Can you explain what this is, and does it relate in any way to your theory?"

MS: "Briefly, technicism is an ideology that became prevalent in the latter half of the twentieth century, particularly after World War II. It is the idea that there is a technological solution to every problem. Dr. el Plasio, pay attention to this. His work involved elucidating the dangers in this idea. Not only did technicism play a role in the rise of the military-industrial complex, but it led to complacency when dealing with problems that have no technological solution. Sociothermodynamics may appear technocratic, but really, the only technocratic part of it is the technology necessary to analyze data. Of course, as I said in the paper, the technological development of a society and its role in that society is one of our variables of interest."

MA₂: "Thank you."

MA₃: "Dr. Stanley, isn't your proposal a roundabout way to get at the problem of 'global warming'? And how do you expect to get funding when this subject has been purged from scientific inquiry because it is said that it doesn't exist?"

MS: "I can tell you are not from the US. The terms 'global warming' and 'climate change' have not only been expunged from the revised official presidential lexicon; they have been expunged from the entire federal government. Although heat is involved in both, my theory has nothing to do with climate science per se. I am aware of the touchiness of this, particularly within the Goldilocks administration, and may have to try to get funding from European sources. I hope one outcome of this conference is a greater awareness of the problem. All I can say is that dissipative heat is the final product of unethical inaction."

MA$_3$: "As an economist, I am appalled that Dr. de Plasio has such a low opinion of my discipline and the social sciences in general. His discipline wouldn't be anywhere without the gifts of finance. Look at all your fancy particle accelerators, gigantic gravity monitors, and all that stuff that is up in space. Finance is the driver of economic growth, without which physics would still be in the Dark Ages."

MeP: "That is simply not true. Basic research is of no interest to financiers. Our funding has come from the government and, now, unfortunately, is at a grave risk of being lost. All financiers have done with their duplicitous financial instruments such as derivatives (that have nothing to do with the derivatives of the calculus) is create havoc that served no purpose except to enrich a few CEOs who didn't bother to complete a college education. Dr. Stanley's theory may be ludicrous, but at least it will be harmless. Finance, on the other hand, can cause real catastrophe."

RA: "I believe that our time is up. I hope all energy involved in this discussion won't end up as wasteful dissipated heat. I want to thank our panelists and Dr. Stanley for her thoughtful paper."

Acknowledgements

The quotations at the beginning of the Epilogue and Appendix are from real people. The goofy sounding experiments performed on the International Space Station are real as documented on NASA's website. Wikipedia was the source for the combustion formulas and the information on oxygen depletion.

www.ingramcontent.com/pod-product-compliance
Lightning Source LLC
Chambersburg PA
CBHW030623130626
46552CB00002B/684